"Corey, Listen To Me,"

Jason spoke urgently, taking a step nearer.

"Don't," she snapped, her hands raised as if to ward him off. "Leave me alone. Don't touch me."

"Don't touch you?" he asked gently, not coming any nearer. "What are you afraid of, Corey? Me? Yourself? Or are you terrified of what we are together?"

"I'm not afraid of anything!"

"Oh, but you are," he countered with a wistful sigh. Jason turned suddenly and strode from the kitchen, stopping only to retrieve his jacket from the coatrack. Standing in the doorway, he glanced over his shoulder at Corey.

"I'm honest enough to admit I want you. And I've seen desire in a woman's eyes too many times not to be able to recognize it. Don't fight the inevitable, Corey. You're merely feeding the fire. And the fire is there, between us. We both know it. We've both felt it. We'll be touched by that fire again and don't you doubt it for one minute!"

Dear Reader:

Series and Spin-offs! Connecting characters and intriguing interconnections to make your head whirl.

In Joan Hohl's successful trilogy for Silhouette Desire— *Texas Gold* (7/86), *California Copper* (10/86), *Nevada Silver* (1/87)—Joan created a cast of characters that just wouldn't quit. You figure out how *Lady Ice* (5/87) connects. And in August, "J.B." demanded his own story—*One Tough Hombre*. In *Falcon's Flight*, coming in November, you'll learn *all* about . . . ?

Annette Broadrick's *Return to Yesterday* (6/87) introduced Adam St. Clair. This August *Adam's Story* tells about the woman who saves his life—and teaches him a thing or two about love!

The six Branigan brothers appeared in Leslie Davis Guccione's *Bittersweet Harvest* (10/86) and *Still Waters* (5/87). September brings *Something in Common*, where the eldest of the strapping Irishmen finds love in unexpected places.

Midnight Rambler by Linda Barlow is in October—a special Halloween surprise, and totally unconnected to anything.

Keep an eye out for other Silhouette Desire favorites— Diana Palmer, Dixie Browning, Ann Major and Elizabeth Lowell, to name a few. You never know when secondary characters will insist on their own story. . . .

All the best,

Isabel Swift
Senior Editor & Editorial Coordinator
Silhouette Books

SHERYL FLOURNOY
Jason's Touch

Silhouette Desire

Published by Silhouette Books New York

America's Publisher of Contemporary Romance

Acknowledgments

Rita Rainville, a dear, wonderful lady who not only takes the time to listen but hears what I am saying.
Beth Rowe, who always answers the phone and saves me from Kennan's answering machine! The lady is a jewel.
Gayle Clabaugh, a friend and confidante who was there with the light of her friendship when the shadows were darkest.

I thank you ladies for your friendship.

SILHOUETTE BOOKS
300 East 42nd St., New York, N.Y. 10017

Copyright © 1987 by Sheryl Hines Flournoy

All rights reserved, including the right to reproduce this book or portions thereof in any form whatsoever. For information address Silhouette Books, 300 East 42nd St., New York, N.Y. 10017

ISBN: 0-373-05371-1

First Silhouette Books printing August 1987

All the characters in this book are fictitious. Any resemblance to actual persons, living or dead, is purely coincidental.

SILHOUETTE, SILHOUETTE DESIRE and colophon are registered trademarks of the publisher.

America's Publisher of Contemporary Romance

Printed in the U.S.A.

Books by Sheryl Flournoy

Silhouette Desire

* *Make No Promises* #8
* *Share Your Tomorrows* #63
Jason's Touch #371

* written as Sherry Dee

SHERYL FLOURNOY

started writing as a result of a dream. She woke up and couldn't remember how it concluded, so she simply wrote her own ending. In regard to her writing, Ms. Flournoy admits she had become "intrigued with the idea of making life what I want it to be...at least for a little while. Writing has become an important part of my life. It's as natural as breathing, and I'm not ready to stop doing either."

Ms. Flournoy began her writing career with Silhouette Books under the pseudonym of Sherry Dee. From there she has gone on to write both contemporary and historical romances, finding the romance genre to be what she loves best.

How shall I do to love? Believe.
How shall I do to believe? Love.

—Leighton

One

"Five minutes, Miss Kelton!"

The call was accompanied by an abrupt knock on the dressing room door, and Corey started, dropping the small jar of stage makeup she was holding. It hit the dressing table with a dull thud; the powder spilled out and rose in a sweet-smelling cloud that drifted across the small space.

Corey had been sitting before the large, brightly lighted makeup mirror, dispassionately studying the image before her. Coughing, she briskly fanned the dust-laden air before her, battling against the slowly settling powder-cloud to get an unrestricted view of the mirror.

With a deep sigh, she leaned forward to give her short, straight nose a quick dusting with the powder puff and put the final touches to her stage makeup.

There had been a time when making this movie had been the most important thing in her career, in her life. But that was before—

"You're wanted on the set, Miss Kelton!" another voice rang out.

"I'm coming!" she replied, a thread of anxiety in her voice.

Corey stood to take one last look at herself. The reflection showed her that the sleek silk gown was molded to every curve of her shapely body and that the deep-cut bodice revealed a good deal of her firm breasts. Her pale skin glistened in the bright lights of the dressing table.

Turning to the door, Corey gripped the doorknob and hesitated. Then, taking a deep breath, she quickly yanked the door open and stepped out into the passageway. A feeling of dread washed over her as she made her way toward the set. *He* would be there, waiting, she thought. Waiting with his amused half smile and his mocking eyes. His presence seemed overpowering, and his arrogant manner greatly annoyed her.

"Well, I won't let him rattle me today," Corey murmured aloud, reassuring herself. "Not today, not tomorrow—*not ever again!*" she vowed angrily, tilted her small chin determinedly and marched purposefully down the short hallway.

"Just pull yourself together," she coached in an undertone. "Show that high and mighty so-and-so that you're strong. Not only can you hold your own, but you have a *mind* of your own!"

Despite her admonition, as the roar of voices met her ears, Corey's feet stopped of their own volition, and she stood rooted to the spot. Her body simply refused to move. But it hadn't been the voices that had affected her this way; it was the sound of that deep, husky laugh that had rumbled across the set. Its velvety sound made Corey's heart leap and her breath quicken.

Why was it that a man she despised could affect her that way? Why did she experience such mixed feelings of anger and fright each time he looked at her with those piercing green eyes? And why did his very presence seem to threaten her, not only as an actress, but as a *woman*.

Again the masculine laughter rang out, and Corey felt her pulse race. Her immediate impulse was to turn and run back down the corridor as fast as her feet could carry her, but before she could move, a heavy hand settled on her shoulder, and Corey jumped. A cry escaped her lips, and she stood still, not daring to turn and discover who was behind her.

"Ready, Corey?"

The warm, familiar voice was soothing to her shattered nerves, and Corey released the breath she was holding and relaxed. Swallowing hard, she stammered, "Y-yes, I'm ready." Slowly she turned toward the speaker and gave the older man a quavering smile.

Cappy Harmon, the director and Corey's longtime friend, stared down at her pale face with grave concern.

"You all right, honey?"

"Yes..." she replied somewhat hesitantly. Then, lifting her slim shoulders as if to throw off a great weight, Corey smiled bravely and said again more firmly, "Yes, Cappy, I'm fine."

"You mustn't let your emotions interfere with your work, love. You're much too good an actress to let that happen." Cappy squeezed her shoulder affectionately. "Banning's a hard man to work with, I know. He's a bit of a perfectionist, but he's fair. He recognizes your talent and your acting ability. He can see your potential, and he's not willing for you to do anything less than your very best. And, yes, he's a strong-willed cuss, even hard at times. But so are you, honey, remember that."

Although Cappy's tone was kindly, his words fell like sharp pebbles. Corey realized the truth of his comments, and they were, in a way, complimentary to her as an actress. Why, then, did she feel even more resentful of Jason Banning than before?

"I'm trying" was all she said as Cappy took her arm firmly and escorted her through the wide doorway labeled Studio 4.

Corey entered the studio reluctantly and stopped just inside the door. Although she didn't look directly at Cappy, she was keenly aware that he was studying her from beneath gray lashes, noting her tenseness.

"You really are afraid of Banning, aren't you?" he asked quietly.

"No!" Corey replied too quickly and too loudly to be convincing, and at Cappy's raised eyebrow, she admitted, "Oh, I don't know, Cappy. I don't think that I really feel anything toward the man other than pure, unadulterated hatred!"

"My dear Corey, the conflict between you and Banning is of your own making. The man—"

At that moment Cappy's name was called from across the room, and he turned to see a young man beckoning to him. Turning briefly back to Corey, he saw the raw emotion in her eyes and wondered just what she was feeling.

Realizing that this was neither the time nor the place to analyze and discuss Corey's feelings, Cappy placed a fatherly arm across her shoulders and together the two made their way through the large barnlike building.

Corey's long gown made it difficult to maneuver, and she was grateful for Cappy's helping hand as they stepped over cables and electric cords, ducked under ladders and small platforms and sidestepped workmen who moved about with cameras, lights and props.

When they reached the set for the day's shooting, Cappy took his place beside one of the cameras, seating himself in the canvas chair bearing the word *Director* in bold letters across its back. Clipboard in hand the young man who had hailed Cappy immediately claimed him in conversation, pointing to the set with his ballpoint pen and making a sweeping gesture.

Corey stood a few feet away, her brown eyes scanning the set with its bedchamber. She took in the massive bed with its wood carvings, the heavy elaborate drapes, the marble fireplace and two large chairs that matched the carved bed.

Her throat felt dry, and her palms became moist. They would be shooting a love scene later this afternoon. She would have to lie upon that bed with *him*, endure *his* embrace, *his* kisses, and speak words of love to him. Smothering the cry that threatened to burst forth, Corey clenched her fists and caught her lower lip between her teeth. She couldn't do it! Although she was an excellent actress, she would never be able to go through with *that* scene. Tears blurred her eyes, and she angrily whisked them away.

Taking a deep breath, she stepped closer to the staged bedroom. As her gaze swept over the comfortable setting, it came to rest on the man sprawled in one of the chairs, his long legs stretched out before him, his booted feet resting on a cushioned footstool. His eyes were closed, and at that moment he looked extremely vulnerable, Corey thought. Her heart stopped its beat then suddenly pounded out of control, and her breath caught in her breast as a tremor coursed through her body.

If ever a man could be described as "beautiful," then that was the word for Jason Banning. "Handsome" seemed too mild a word. He reminded her of a modern Apollo. An exquisite, flawless work of art that its creator had carefully carved from marble, then breathed life into, causing the subject to become vibrantly alive.

The only thing that marred this work of perfection, Corey decided, was a thread-thin scar about an inch long that ran beneath and parallel with the right side of his lower lip. But that flaw certainly did nothing to detract from the man: it merely enhanced his virile appearance and good looks.

Corey studied the man before her with undisguised interest. His hair was thick, a rich, warm brown with copper highlights, and it hung carelessly about the nape of his neck. He had deeply etched features, his jaw strong, his mouth sensuous and often curved in a lazy half-crooked smile. His straight nose and determined chin both portrayed extreme self-confidence, power and arrogance.

Yes, Corey admitted to herself, Jason Banning was far more than handsome. And, she was further forced to admit, he held an undeniable attraction for her that she fought constantly. Her gaze traveled slowly over his deeply sun-kissed skin, his broad shoulders and chest, his long, muscular legs. His very being seemed to exude an authority that not merely asked for but demanded respect.

Suddenly aware that Jason had opened his eyes and that his brilliant emerald-green stare was upon her, Corey felt a rush of heat engulf her, yet she couldn't tear her eyes from his.

Mesmerized, she watched as Jason slowly and gracefully rose from the chair and strode forward to stand in front of her, his eyes shining, amusement in their cool depths.

"If you continue to look at me like that," he told her softly, "I'll be obliged to respond to the passion I see smoldering in your eyes."

The words snapped Corey out of her trance as surely as if Jason had dumped a pail of ice-cold water on her head. Anger rose swiftly within her, and she clenched her hands into tight fists at her sides as she felt the strong urge to slap his smug face. She longed to hurl a cutting retort at him but instead just stood there, her mouth pressed into a thin line, her flashing tawny eyes held in silent combat with his.

What in heaven's name was wrong with her? How could she just stand here and let him get by with such a blatantly

suggestive remark? He had boldly declared that she was is-
suing a silent invitation, a declaration of attraction to him.
Disgusting! The nerve, the unmitigated gall of the man!

"At a loss for words, Miss Kelton?" Jason taunted in a
low, husky voice as he moved closer and reached confidently for her.

"Don't touch me!" Corey choked out. She tried to sound
forceful and convincing, but her voice was just above a
whisper. She realized that she was trembling, and her knees
felt weak, as if they might suddenly buckle beneath her.

Banning smiled knowingly and, lifting one dark brow,
moved closer but did not touch her. "A femme fatale," he
murmured seductively. "You stir a man's passion and
awaken his desire just by the way you look and move."
Without warning, Jason reached out and tenderly ran his
fingers over the silkiness of her cheek, causing Corey's
breath to still. "You challenge a man's masculinity with
your cool indifference and wreak havoc with his senses."

The throatiness of his voice, the warmth and gentleness
of his touch against her skin both stirred and frightened her,
and Corey fought the magnetic pull of his words even as
they aroused her emotions. She wouldn't get caught in this
man's trap, she vowed, despising him for his arrogance and
self-assurance.

She tried to speak, but found that she could not.

"I want to unleash the passion I can sense within you,"
Banning went on. "A passion I feel sure no one else has
discovered." He stroked her cheek with a hypnotic rhythm.

"Never!" Corey suddenly found her voice, and she
hurled the one word at him with such intensity that it caused
a few heads to turn in their direction.

"Ah, Corey, don't be so quick to protest," Jason cautioned softly. "I'm a man who makes a point of getting
what he wants. Consider yourself fairly warned." He

dropped his hand from her cheek and smiled disarmingly before walking away.

Corey stared after him, but before she could make a fitting rejoinder, Cappy's voice rang out. "Ready on the set!"

Corey made her way to the false window and looked out, taking a deep breath. Resolutely she steadied her shaking hands, stiffened her back and made a desperate attempt to regain her composure.

Her emotions were seething within her, and she knew that if she pulled off the following scene, the greatest performance of her life would occur in the next few minutes. She had to recover from the emotional upheaval Jason had caused and carry on as if he had never hinted that there could be anything between them.

"Ready, Corey?" Cappy called out. When she gave no answer, he repeated loudly, "Corey! Are you ready?" When she mutely nodded her head, he called to the others. "All right, everybody, take your places. Quiet on the set . . . and ROLL!"

Cameras began whirring, and the scene got underway.

The door burst open, and Jason, playing the role of Miles Carver, stalked in, his face flushed with anger.

"How *dare* you walk out on me!" he roared at the woman standing before the window. "Judith, you will return to the ball at my side—"

"I will go *no*where with you, Miles!" Corey replied with spirit, in her role of Judith.

"The hell you won't!" Miles bellowed as he crossed the room and yanked her by the arm. "You will not embarrass me—humiliate me—before my friends!"

"Humiliate *you*?" Judith countered heatedly. "What about *me*? I saw you and that . . . that Sheldon hussy!" She laughed bitterly. "You were far too involved to notice that I was on the balcony! So let me tell you what you can do—"

He crushed her against his powerful chest, robbing her of breath. His face was a mere breath from her own.

"Woman, you go too far!" The words were hissed through clenched teeth. "You will tell me nothing! I am master here, and you will do my bidding!"

"Release me!" she screamed, struggling in his steely arms, kicking out at him with her slipper-clad foot. "Take your filthy hands off me!" She broke free of his hold and stepped back. "Don't keep the *lady* waiting, go back to Norma Sheldon and pick up where you left off! Caress her body, take *her* to your bed! *I want no part of you, Jason Banning!*" And at those words, Corey raised her hand and slapped Jason a stinging blow across his cheek.

Neither her final declaration nor the slap were in the script—and Corey had called Jason by his own name, rather than the name of the character he was portraying. Stunned, Cappy and and the cast stared speechlessly, watching the events before them.

Completely oblivious to the spellbound audience, the scene between Jason and Corey continued. Dangerous glints flickered in the depths of Banning's green eyes, and Corey's heart hammered in her breast. The spark of electricity flared between them, and their eyes met, clashed and held, each determined not to yield. There was tremendous tension in Jason's body and a warning tautness in the straight line of his mouth.

Corey realized her mistake, knew that Jason was like a coiled snake, readying to strike, but her body seemed reluctant to respond to the command of her brain to flee from this angry man.

"It had to come to this," Jason said in a low voice. A lazy smile touched his lips, and in one step he closed the gap between them. "I knew right from the beginning that you would provoke me to this point, and now you've done it."

He crushed Corey to his hard body, bent his dark head, and with a ragged curse he took her lips in a hungry kiss, taking possession of her mouth.

"I'll tame you," Jason whispered against her lips, his breath warm, his voice husky. "Be warned, Corey. I'll break your resistance, melt your ice and set you aflame with the need of me."

Fury swept over her, and Corey tried to push Jason away, but he only tightened his hold and deepened the kiss, demanding and arousing a response. Corey could hardly breathe, and her protest was only a choked sound in her throat.

Jason held her tightly before breaking the kiss and standing her away from him. He smiled triumphantly down into her flushed face, noting the heaving of her full breasts and the unsteadiness of her stance.

Every nerve in Corey's body seemed to quiver, and her glazed eyes met those of Jason before he allowed his gaze to roam without haste over her slender frame, coming to rest upon her slightly parted lips, still moist from his kiss. With a quick move he reached out to trace her soft mouth, his thumb slowly, seductively following the outline of her tender lips.

Corey stood transfixed under his knowing gaze, unable to voice the thoughts that were running through her head. She was incapable of ignoring the heat, the stirring in her blood that his touch and the taste of his lips had generated.

At the sound of approaching footsteps the spell was broken, and they turned to see Cappy coming toward them. Only then were they made aware of the fact that the cameras had ceased to roll and that the eyes of every member of the cast and crew were fastened on the two of them.

"It's been a long, tiring day, Cappy," Jason addressed the older man, gaining control of the situation. "I think both Miss Kelton and I need a break from the pressures of this project. And, I might add, Miss Kelton definitely needs to study her script, as she most certainly digressed from her lines." He gave Corey a sidelong glance, laughing quietly at her indrawn breath.

"H-how dare you! You arrogant, conceited son—" Corey flared, choking on her words in her anger.

"Yes, yes," Cappy broke in, his hand settling on her shoulder. "Jason is right. We all need a break." He glanced at his watch and called across the set, "Lunch! Half hour!"

Corey glared mutinously from Jason to Cappy. Rage, embarrassment—unnamed emotions gripped her. Unwilling to allow the others to see the state she was in, she turned and walked with measured tread across the set, headed for the privacy of her dressing room. Her body was tense and tears threatened behind her brown eyes.

The sound of Cappy's voice followed her, and she heard him apologizing to Jason for the delay, asking pardon for *her*! Hot tears stung her eyes, and when she reached her destination, Corey's eyes were swimming, and her mind was in a turmoil. She couldn't believe the recent events. The encounter with Jason was bad enough, but why had Cappy taken sides with her enemy? Why did he feel it necessary to pacify Jason Banning?

After all, Jason wasn't flawless. *He* was at fault, as well: the man was forever harassing her and had finally pushed her to the limit. It was true that she'd blown her lines and interrupted the shoot, but his comments that had followed, the embrace, the kiss—

Corey shook her head in an effort to clear her mind of the memory of Jason's arms about her, his lips on hers.

She sank heavily into the chair before her dressing table. In her absence someone had dimmed the lights surrounding the large mirror, and she stared into the shadowed glass. Who was the young woman staring back at her? The eyes were the same dark brown as her own, yet they no longer danced with excitement. They were sad eyes, their usual golden sparks shadowed. The lips that so readily smiled were now tremulous, and the small chin quivered.

Corey's nerves were too tightly strung, and there was too much on her mind to concentrate on her work or do justice to her acting. She would never be able to work with Jason Banning! No matter how hard she tried, she was unable to put aside her intense dislike of the man. From their first meeting they had never agreed on *anything*! And she could never forgive him for what he had done to Matt. For that reason alone she hated the man.

Matt. How was she to go on without him? A sob caught in her throat at the thought of dear Matt. Her heart held a dull ache, an emptiness, and her mind was clouded with thoughts of Matt's death.

Folding her arms on the table's smooth surface, Corey rested her weary head within their cradle, sighing heavily. Memories flooded her, and she began to relive the past....

Eight years before, Corey's parents had been taken from her suddenly, tragically, leaving her with no family to comfort her, for they were all she had. At sixteen she had been strong in spite of her fears, and outwardly had borne up under her grief as an adult while the child inside was crying out with the need of compassion and understanding.

A lifelong friend of her family, Matt Fielder had taken her into his heart and become her family as her beloved parents had entrusted him to do. He had assured her that life would go on, that although the pain was raw and piercing, it would eventually diminish and settle in a private place in her heart. He had cared for her, loved her, given her hope and guidance.

Matt owned Fielder Studios, where Corey's mother had been under contract. Livia Kelton had been one of the most sought-after actresses of her time. Corey's father, Griff, a famous screenwriter and director, had been Matt's best friend. It was only natural that Corey should pursue a career in the film industry.

And here she was again, the pain of death once more fresh and raw within her heart, but no Matt to comfort her this time. Matt had left her, and God, how it hurt! She felt the fears, the unanswered questions acutely. Although her parents' death had been an accident, Matt had taken his own life. That was what was so hard for her to understand, so difficult to accept.

What was done was done, and there was no changing the fact, yet Corey's hatred and bitterness had grown. She couldn't put the past behind her. Matt had been in deep financial trouble and had been about to lose the studios. He had needed help, but when he'd turned to his "friends" he found none that were willing to help.

As a last resort he had turned to Jason Banning, the son of Matt's close friend who had died the year before. Matt had been there for his friend when the older Banning had desperately needed both a friend and money. But the son of that friend had refused to return the favor.

When no one else would help Matt save the studios, Corey had given him the better part of her savings, as had their friend and ally, Cappy Harmon. Because they had so willingly given up their savings to rescue Fielder Studios and because of their belief in him, Matt had told Corey and Cappy that, should anything happen to him, the studios would be left to the two of them. Soon afterward, the studio had begun to thrive after an uphill struggle and, once again, all had been well.

Then Matt Fielder had committed suicide!

This is all a nightmare, Corey thought now in the dimness of her dressing room, wishing she would wake up and see Matt smiling at her from across the room. Yes, if Matt were only here, everything would be fine, she reasoned. But

Matt would never again be here with her, never again be here to set things right.

Oh, how she wished . . .

"You have to face reality," she said suddenly, scolding the image before her. "Remember what Cappy said, *'Matt is gone!* This is *not* just a dream, Corey!'"

A small sob caught in her throat, and tears misted her eyes anew as she gave way to the painful ache within her.

Two

It had been a most trying week, culminating with the hectic topsy-turvy day she'd survived yesterday, and Corey wanted nothing more to do with the hated script, Cappy's wishes or Jason Banning. All she wanted to do was to escape the studio and all that it represented.

But so much time had been lost already—precious time that *she* had been blamed for wasting—that Corey felt she had no choice but to carry on, to finish the day's work in order to keep within the schedule. No one cared that she was utterly emotionally drained, that she would rather be anywhere than where she was at this moment, doing anything other than what she was doing.

They were working on a torrid love scene, a scene that should be played with heated passion and stark intensity, yet Corey wasn't able to play the scene as it should be. Jason's nearness disturbed her, his voice grated on her senses, and his touch seared her flesh, making her all too aware of him as a desirable man. She was fighting a losing battle against her emotions and her rising attraction to him.

"Come on, Corey, for Christ's sake! This is supposed to be a *love* scene!" Cappy's voice boomed across the large studio, and Corey's gaze met his with a silent plea in her warm brown eyes. Couldn't he see just how hard this was for her? He knew her feelings toward the despised Jason Banning. How could she *possibly* do a convincing love scene? Every time Jason put his arms around her, brought her close to his powerful body, his lips—

"Corey!"

The urgent call of her name jolted her to attention, bringing her from her wanderings, and she looked up at the man who stopped before her.

"Cappy, I'm trying!"

"Oh, *are* you?" There was no mistaking the sarcasm in his voice.

"Honest, I am!" she told him, her hands outstretched, appealing for his understanding.

"I know better," Cappy said in a gentler tone, his eyes holding hers. "I've seen you act before, Corey. Even on a bad day and with an atrocious script, I've seen you do better."

"Miss Kelton." Jason's deep voice rumbled from just behind her, and Corey started. "I'm enjoying this even less than you are, I can assure you."

Corey turned to look at the source of her discomfiture as he continued nonchalantly, "But they are a *must*, the love scenes. After all, this *is* a love story. The script is written, we each have our roles, and there's a lot of time, as well as money, invested in this project."

As he paused, Corey felt herself flush heatedly under his steady gaze. How dare he! She would give him his due, she decided, but before she could counter, Jason looked at her through narrowed green eyes and continued in a slow, deliberate tone.

"The longer it takes you to do this scene right, the more time and money you cost this company."

"Mister Banning!" Corey returned spiritedly, "I'm very well aware of all the facts. You needn't point them out! I think you should—"

"Might I remind you that I'm doing *my* part, Miss Kelton?" he broke in haughtily. "The director has no complaint with me. As a professional, I've always found that *I* could put petty dislikes and personality clashes aside. If you're set on being an actress—a *professional*—I suggest that you learn to do the same."

"Don't you *dare* stand there so—so condescending and tell me what to do!" Corey bit out, her temper flaring. She lunged forward, her finger jabbing at his broad chest. "Just who do you think you are?" she demanded, her lovely face flushing in her anger. She drew a deep breath and was about to continue when Cappy's voice cut her short.

"Good God! What is it with you two? Will you please— Oh, what the hell," he moaned, throwing his hands up and shaking his steel-gray head. Then, pointing at the young woman, he ordered, "Come to my office, Corey, *now!*"

Cappy turned abruptly on his heel and strode from the studio, mumbling over his shoulder that everyone should take a break.

Corey stood stiffly for a long moment, her fists clenched at her sides. Her golden-brown eyes locked with the cool, emerald gaze of Jason in silent combat. How she hated him, this man who stood towering over her with his superior air. How she'd love to slap that smirk off his face!

Jason's full lips spread in a slow smile. Then he threw back his dark head and laughed, and the vibrant sound sent a shudder through Corey's body and warmed her blood.

"Called down in class, Miss Kelton?" Jason asked mockingly. With a small, subtle movement of his head he indicated the direction of Cappy's office. "Better run along."

Inwardly seething, Corey met his gaze with a determined fire sparking her tawny eyes, and she tilted her chin upward. A sudden disarming smile touched her lips and, without warning, Miss Kelton punched the unsuspecting Jason Banning in his flat, well-muscled stomach with her clenched fist!

His sudden *ouf* as his breath was expelled and the stunned surprise that lit his eyes were immensely gratifying. She smiled and turned gracefully to saunter away with all the dignity of royalty, leaving a cursing, yet intrigued Jason in her wake.

Still maintaining her regal bearing, Corey entered Cappy's office and calmly closed the door behind her. Once assured that the wooden barrier was between her and the arrogant Jason, relieved that he hadn't followed her, she released the breath that she had been unconsciously holding.

"Sit down, Corey," Cappy instructed, pointing to the high-backed leather chair beside his desk.

"I don't need a lecture, Cappy," she declared as she flopped into a chair. "You, of all people, should understand. You know how I feel about Jason Banning. How can you expect me to—"

"I expect you to be an actress, Corey," Cappy broke in, "nothing less!"

"I am *trying* to be nothing less!" she cried passionately, jumping up. "God, how I'm trying. Ohhh, I just want to scream!" She raised a fist into the air and hissed through clenched teeth, "Oh, I just want to hit something. I—I want to slug Jason Banning, the pompous toad!"

Slug him? Isn't that what she had just done? What on earth had possessed her to do such a thing? Although she had fairly itched to, she hadn't dreamed she'd actually do it. She had actually slugged Jason! The realization suddenly came crashing down upon her, and her laughter burst forth, giving vent to excess emotion and frustration.

Cappy looked at her as if she had lost her mind.

"And that's just what I did," Corey announced, and her laughter rang out once more—until she saw the stunned disbelief on Cappy's face.

"You *what*?"

"I slugged him! Gave him a mean right hook to his belly. Knocked the breath right out of him." She sat down and studied her fingernails with great interest.

"You didn't!" Cappy denied unbelievingly, leaping from his perch on the corner of the desk.

"Oh, but I did!"

Cappy stared at Corey and saw the bald truth shining in her eyes. He couldn't help smiling, wishing he could have seen it for himself. She had always been a little spitfire, having a temper that flared when least expected, and he knew her well enough to expect the unexpected.

"Did you hurt him?" Cappy couldn't help but ask.

"I sure hope I did!"

"Now, Corey," he began in a soothing voice.

"Don't you 'now, Corey,' me, Cappy Harmon! I hate the man! I can't work with him. I *won't* work with him. I want out of this picture!" Corey began pacing the room like a caged animal.

"Corey, you don't really mean that."

"Oh, but I do!" she returned hotly.

"You wanted this part. You read the script, and you're perfect for the role. My God, you know what Matt went through to assure you this part!"

"Matt is dead!" she slammed back at Cappy, her words filled with emotion. "D E A D! Remember? You keep telling me to face that fact."

"Have you, honey?" he asked quietly. "Is it acceptance, or is it just your anger I'm hearing?"

"Anger, pain, confusion—isn't each of them alone, as well as all of them combined, part of facing the facts?" she asked in a flat, lifeless voice and sank back into the chair. Tears threatened, and in a choked voice she repeated, "Matt is dead and I have accepted his death. He is gone, thanks to his so-called friends and the likes of Jason Banning! And you expect me to rub elbows day in and day out with the man, follow through with passionate love scenes and act as if I'm indifferent to what has happened?

"I'm sorry, Cappy. I would do just about anything for you, but *that* I cannot do! I'll never forgive Jason Banning for what he did to Matt! Never! And I won't do this picture with him."

Again the distraught young woman rose from the chair and, whisking a tattletale tear from her eye, continued in a pain-filled voice, "I refuse to be held by him, kissed by him, and I won't speak words of love to him. I don't want to be in the same room with him, much less play his game and act as if nothing has happened. I won't tolerate him, not even for the sake of this movie."

"Corey, you can't blame Jason for what happened to Matt."

"Can't I?" she spat, slamming her hands flat upon the desk top.

"Jason had nothing to do with his death, nor did his friends. Matt was weak and frightened. He still had money problems, Corey. The threat of losing the studios was still very much a reality. I know you don't want to hear anything against him, Corey, but you have to face *all* the facts.

"Matt Fielder was one of my best friends; I loved him, but I can't close my eyes to the truth. I won't allow you to do it, either. He's gone, and there's not a day that goes by that I don't feel the loss. I feel it every bit as much as you do," Cappy went on honestly, with a catch in his voice. He reached out to clasp Corey's hands within his and spoke in a low, gentle whisper.

"You say that you accept his death, Corey, but it's just so many words, and they're empty ones. You're saying them, but you're not believing them. What good is that?"

Cappy watched the play of emotions on her lovely face, saw the tears shimmering in her eyes. She was still fighting with herself. "Accept Matt's death, Corey, and let him go. We don't always understand the reasons for the actions of those we love. That fact can blind us and make us bitter. It'll destroy you if you allow it to." He sighed wearily. "Accept that which cannot be changed, Corey. Not Jason, not anyone other than Matt himself, put that gun to his head, Corey."

Corey removed her hands from Cappy's and moved to the window, gazing out unseeingly. A brief, poignant silence followed. Then, taking a deep, ragged breath, she spoke just above a whisper. "I have to get away for a while, Cappy. I have to deal with this in my own way, on my own time. As for working with Jason, that's something I can't deal with, at all. You'll either have to find a replacement for me or replace Jason."

"Banning won't agree to that alternative. He isn't going to like this, not at all. He's—"

"I don't give a damn what Banning likes or dislikes!" Corey hurled the words across the room as she spun around to face her friend. The hostility in her voice shocked the man. "Fielder Studios doesn't answer to Jason Banning! This is *our* studio, Cappy. Matt left it to you and me. We have the say."

"Honey, there's something I think you should know. Jason—"

"Not another word about that man!" Corey cut in angrily. "He's the one who should be replaced," she decided abruptly. "Why should I give up my role? It means a lot to me and to my career. I've made my decision, Cappy, and as head of Fielder Studios—"

"As head of Fielder Studios, what?" the amused voice of Jason came from behind her. Startled, she rounded on the man who filled the doorway with his tall, commanding frame, his mere presence dominating the room.

Caught up in her tirade, Corey hadn't heard the door open. As always, their gazes locked in silent battle. They stood at odds as an uneasy quiet claimed the room.

"Er, Jason," Cappy stammered in confusion as he rose from his seat. "Corey is somewhat upset. She, well, she's not been herself since—"

"Corey can speak for herself!" she announced flatly. "You needn't feel as if you have to make excuses for me, Cappy. I'm quite capable of telling Mr. Banning what I just told you."

"Please do," Jason invited.

"Corey, I—" Cappy's words were cut off by the look she darted at him and by Jason's raised hand, motioning him to be silent.

"I'd like to hear what Miss Kelton has to say to me."

Jason's cool tone caused Cappy to close his eyes tightly, and his lips moved as if in silent prayer.

The younger man crossed his arms over his broad chest, leaned casually against the doorjamb and pinned Corey with his emerald gaze as he waited for her to speak.

"I refuse to continue this picture with you as leading man, Mr. Banning. I find that there are too many conflicts—differences of opinion—and, let's face it, we both know there is a definite personality clash between you and me," Corey informed him coldly. "Furthermore, I feel that—that is…well, to put it bluntly, I don't like you the least bit, and in short, I find it impossible to work with you."

"'To put it bluntly,' are you suggesting that the studio replace me as leading man?" he queried, raising one dark eyebrow. He cocked his head to one side as if to look at her from a different angle, then, without giving her time to answer, he continued. "Both the producers and the director, as well as myself, are pleased with my performance in the picture, Miss Kelton. I have no intention of stepping out of the role and no intention of being replaced."

"This studio may feel differently," Corey informed him with a haughty tilt of her chin, her brown eyes shooting angry golden sparks. "And, as you well know, Mr. Banning, the studio owners have quite a lot to say about the matter."

"Corey, honey—" Once again Cappy attempted to break into the verbal fencing, but he found himself completely ignored.

"And, as one of the owners of Fielder Studios," Corey went on, oblivious to Cappy's words, "I can and will demand your replacement!"

Corey was completely unaware of the low groan that came from Cappy as he placed the palm of one hand over his weary blue eyes. She was aware only of the puzzling smile on Jason's lips as he lounged carelessly in the open door.

With a catlike movement, Jason reached for the door with one tanned hand and pushed it shut behind him. He walked purposefully across the room, passed Corey without a glance and went around the desk to take the chair that Cappy had hastily vacated. Seating himself, Banning leaned forward to place his loosely clasped hands on the polished desk and tapped his thumbs together as he studied the watchful young woman, considering her thoughtfully.

His action roused Corey to further anger. What right did this man have to act as if he were the one in control? Had it anything to do with what Cappy had tried to tell her and to which she'd refused to listen. Now the words "There's something I think you should know" were echoing in her mind. Did Jason have more to do with the picture than she knew about?

As she observed the confident man across he desk, his dark eyes holding a knowing look, Corey realized that her words hadn't threatened him in the least. There was a sudden awakening of alarm within her and a feeling of cold dread washed over her.

"Be seated, Miss Kelton," Jason instructed.

"I prefer to stand," she retorted icily, rebelling against his peremptory manner and resentful of his authoritative tone of voice.

"Fine by me," came his rejoinder, accompanied by an indifferent shrug of his broad shoulders. "Now, to return to the matter of our controversy, I have to say that your opinion doesn't matter in the least. You can say anything you want to anyone you want, demand my replacement, threaten, cajole, but it'll all be of absolutely no consequence, Miss Kelton. The bottom line is that I'll remain as the leading man, and *you*, darlin', *will* continue your role as leading lady." His tone brooked no argument. "You see, Corey, I don't give a damn whether you like or dislike me, and I don't care a whit about your demands."

Corey drew in a sharp breath at his bald statement, and her gaze sought Cappy's but found no sympathy. She opened her mouth to protest, but Jason spoke again.

"You will—"

"I will do nothing!" she interrupted furiously. "Nothing that *you* tell me to do. I won't answer to you. You don't own me!"

"No?" he replied with amusement, his eyebrow quirked.

"No!"

"Think again, my lovely spitfire." Reaching into the desk, Jason retrieved a manila folder and slapped it onto the desk top, one tanned finger jabbing at the label. "*This* says I do. Your contract, Miss Kelton."

She didn't understand what he was saying. As an owner of the studios, *she* owned her contract—not Jason Banning.

"Fielder Studios owns my contract," Corey informed him with controlled politeness, although no longer sure of herself.

"You're right, Corey, and Fielder Studios is now a part of, and owned by, Banning Productions." His words were spoken matter-of-factly.

Corey stared wide-eyed and openmouthed. What was he saying? How could he—

"I see you're confused. Please allow me to enlighten you. *I* own this studio, as well as all other Fielder holdings. I own the existing scripts, rights and contracts of every actor and actress contracted to Fielder. I own it all, Miss Kelton, right down to the lead in the last pencil."

Corey's shocked eyes looked wildly in Cappy's direction.

The kindly old man had remained silent throughout the exchange. Now he met Corey's frantic questioning gaze, and the pain within their golden depths cut his heart like a knife. In answer to her unspoken question, Cappy merely nodded his gray head in mute acknowledgment.

"Cappy, why didn't you—" The words were a choked sound, and Corey broke off the question, realizing that the man had tried to tell her something that she hadn't been willing to hear.

"I tried, honey. You wouldn't listen."

Dragging her eyes from the miserable look in the eyes of her dearest friend and clutching the shreds of her shattered dignity about her like a cloak, Corey faced Jason, eyeing him warily.

"A contract, Miss Kelton, is a binding agreement between two or more parties. It is enforced by law and cannot be dissolved prematurely. Except, of course, by mutual consent of all parties involved."

"I'm well aware of the facts," Corey responded with a disdainful toss of her head. "However, you are here and now advised that *this* party does not choose to continue her contract with Fielder Studios, now that it is a part of Banning Productions, for this party does not wish to have any dealings with its owner."

"And *you*, Miss Kelton, may be advised that *this* party chooses not to release you from said contract."

Leaning back in his chair, Jason lazily crossed his hands behind his dark head and boldly appraised the beautiful young woman before him, watching the mixed feelings that played across her lovely face.

His green eyes made a slow assessment of Corey from her honey-brown hair falling free about her shoulders to her small, slipper-clad feet. His keen eyes noted her sharply defined features, the tawny-brown eyes fringed with golden lashes, her soft lips. A smile touched Jason's own lips at the flush that stole over her face at his open scrutiny.

Ignoring her discomfort and embarrassment, Jason continued his deliberate contemplation of Corey's physical attributes. Jason summed up Corey as he had the first time he had seen her and realized that his opinion hadn't changed. Miss Corey Kelton was indeed sexy, mysterious, spirited and extremely exciting!

Chuckling to himself, he remembered her punch. He liked a woman with fire. A hot temper could only mean tempered passion, and Lord, how he would love to taste her passion! She was willful, spoiled and much too confident. He would greatly enjoy the chase, Jason admitted to himself, and he would find a great deal of satisfaction in taming the free spirit within her.

Prompted by his thoughts, Jason drawled, "I'm going to enjoy working with you, Corey. It'll be a pleasure to teach you to rein in that fiery temper of yours. Taming you will be quite a task."

"You won't have the opportunity to 'tame' me, Mr. Banning, and you needn't concern yourself with my temper, for I won't be around," she spat with undisguised venom.

"Oh? But you have no recourse," Jason countered confidently. "You do remember your contract?"

"I'm sure I don't have to tell you what you can do with that contract!" Corey returned in a throaty purr with a steely undertone. "I'm not afraid of you, your money, or your position, Jason Banning—so, sue me!" Corey flung the words at him and turned to leave.

"Sue you, hell!" Jason exploded, leaping and overturning his chair in his fury.

He came around the desk with lightning speed, and Corey was brought to a sudden, abrupt halt when his powerful hands seized her upper arms. His grip, as it closed about her tender flesh, was like the jaws of a steel trap closing about its helpless prey.

Corey cried out, then stood frozen and trembling before him. His handsome face was a mask of suppressed fury. She stared into the stormy jade eyes that held her captive and fought to keep from being pulled into their fathomless depths. He reminded her of an angered bull, readying to charge, feeling the need to trample its tormentor into the dust.

"Sue you, Corey?" he said in a steely voice as his lips hovered dangerously close to her own. "I'll ruin you!" he whispered, his breath mingling with hers.

Corey pulled free of his hold and, with a choked cry, fled from the room—fled from Jason Banning.

Three

———

As the shadows of evening crept in, Corey's apartment was hushed and still, except for the steady hum of the ceiling fan and the low murmur of the television.

Corey lay motionless, staring unseeingly, her eyes red-rimmed and swollen from hours of crying. Now a shudder passed through her body and, taking a long, ragged breath, she hugged closer the pillow she clutched.

Emotionally drained, she felt numb, except for her heart, which ached almost unbearably. She longed for someone to hold her, comfort and console her. How she needed someone to make the pain go away!

But there was no one. She was terribly alone, and the loneliness so acute that it tore at her. A dark void threatened to consume her, to pull her into its depths of nothingness.

Corey didn't even remember the drive home from the studio. From the moment of the confrontation with Jason when she'd learned the fate of the studios, she had been sucked into a vacuum of roiling emotional turmoil and confusion. She had run from the studio and Jason Banning. It was a miracle that she hadn't had an accident driving the ten miles from the studio to her apartment.

Vaguely she remembered that as she had fumbled with her keys to her apartment building a neighbor had passed her. She had stepped through the front door, wiping tears from her eyes, and assured the woman that she was all right, saying that she had just had a bad day.

But by the time she had reached the privacy of her fourth floor apartment, she had fallen apart, flinging her purse and keys to fall where they may. She fled to her bedroom and threw herself across the bed, sobbing uncontrollably.

As if from a great distance, she had heard the persistent ringing of the telephone and once heard someone knock on her door but had ignored both. Now, as she lay spent in the aftermath of her emotional outburst, she wondered idly who had tried to reach her. But the thought was followed by an indifferent shrug. What did it really matter?

Once again the shrill ringing of the telephone shattered the quiet, but Corey simply stared at the offending instrument. Having no desire to speak to a soul, she chose not to answer. In fact, at the moment she wondered if she would *ever* wish to see or speak to *anyone* ever again. She wanted to shut out the whole world! She wanted to crawl deep into the shadows of some safe place where she didn't have to think, feel, or care. She was tired of being hurt, tired of disappointment—she was tired of everything!

"What is life, after all?" Corey asked aloud. "I had only a few brief years of happiness before I lost my mother and father. My world was shattered until dear Matt, with his understanding and unending patience, helped me to start over again and feel that I belonged."

She lay quietly for a few moments as her thoughts ran on, then again spoke into the silence. "But now Matt is gone, the studio is gone and, with it, the bulk of my savings. And you, Corey Kelton, have just walked out on your contract and the juiciest plum of a part you've ever had! So where does that leave you?" she asked herself, her hands outspread in a gesture of emptiness and defeat.

A dry, rasping sob tore from her throat, but there were no more tears. Her eyes felt dry and hot, and she rose from the bed to strip her clothes.

She walked into the bathroom and turned on the water. A shower would refresh her, and perhaps she could pull herself together enough to think. Glancing into the mirror, Corey groaned at the sight that greeted her. Her face was flushed from crying, her eyes were red and puffy, and her nose was rosy.

Stepping into the shower, she welcomed the cool spray. How she wished she could wash away all her pain, all her troubles and problems, as easily as washing her tired body. But then no one ever said life was easy or that things would go as you wanted them to.

After her bath Corey slipped into an emerald silk wrap and towel-dried her hair. Then, tossing the towel to a nearby chair, she padded barefoot to the kitchen. She stood before the open refrigerator, looking disinterestedly at its contents.

With a heavy sigh she closed the door, moved to the large pantry and retrieved a tin of spiced tea. At the stove she placed a kettle of water to heat and walked again to stare at the inside of her fridge.

The shrilling whistle of the kettle signaled that the water was boiling and brought Corey's wandering thoughts back to the present.

Halfheartedly she poured the water into an oversize earthen mug and dropped a silver tea ball into the steaming liquid. Then she sat down at the bar that divided the kitchen and breakfast room to nibble absently on the cold chicken breast she had finally decided on.

Realizing that she had no interest in food, she wondered why she was wasting her time attempting to eat. She pushed the plate aside and stood to brew more tea. Cup in hand, she left the kitchen, turning off lights and the television as she ambled without purpose through the apartment.

The rational part of Corey's brain warned her that she was rambling, both mentally and physically. But the irrational, unconcerned part told her that it really didn't matter.

Again the ringing of the telephone broke the quiet, and Corey stopped in the doorway of the bedroom, her fingers tightening on the warm mug she cupped in her hand.

"I've had enough of you," she muttered at the annoying object as it continued to ring. "*More* than enough!"

With quick strides she crossed the bedroom to stand over the telephone and, when it stopped ringing, reached down and removed the receiver from its cradle. Opening the top drawer of the bedside table, she placed the receiver inside, muffled it with sweatshirt and closed the drawer.

After one last sip of tea, she placed the mug on the table and pulled back the patchwork down comforter on the bed. She crawled between the cool sheets and turned off the bedside lamp. A glance at the clock showed the time to be a few minutes before midnight. As she settled back against the softness of the pillow, Corey again felt the hot sting of tears that had sprung unbidden to her eyes.

"No! You've got to stop this infernal blubbering," she chided herself. "Stop wallowing in self-pity! You're stronger than this, you *have* to be!"

She had always been a fighter—so where was that fighting spirit now? Hadn't she always fought for the ones she loved, for the things she wanted, for what was hers? This

was just a moment of weakness; wasn't everyone entitled to
an occasional temporary lapse of self-confidence?

Restless, she shifted about in the bed, trying to get comfortable, pounding the pillow in an attempt to fluff it, kicking at the restraining covers on her feet. Finally she rolled
onto her stomach and buried her bright head under the pillow.

"Oh, Dad!" she whispered miserably. "What should I
do? Where can I turn?"

The memory of her father came to her mind. Griff Kelton had been a strong man and had instilled strength of
character in his only child. Suddenly Corey became angry.
She sat upright in bed, her breath coming short and fast.

"If you think I'm going to take what has happened without so much as putting up a fight, Jason Banning, you've
got another think coming!" she said aloud. Then, remembering his words, she added, "I'm not going to have my
spirit tamed by the likes of *you*! It'll take a better man than
you to achieve that colossal task!"

Her mind's eye conjured up the scene earlier, and she remembered with pleasure the satisfaction she'd felt when
she'd punched Jason. "That wasn't, the final blow, Mr.
Banning, by far," she vowed with feeling and smiled into the
darkness. "Not by far!"

The ringing of the alarm clock finally penetrated her deep
sleep, and Corey peeked up from the corner of the pillow
under which her head was buried. Sleepily she groped for
the clock and fumbled with the buttons until she found the
one to silence the irritating noise.

After a few moments Corey threw aside the pillow, rolled
over on her back and stretched lazily. She stared upward at
the slowly revolving ceiling fan, and the monotony of the
steadily rotating blades seemed to have a hypnotic effect on
her.

Her thoughts turned again to the past, and memories scurried around and around in her head. She could almost hear her father's voice. *"Never be a quitter, honey. Never allow yourself to be cornered, but* should *that happen, come out of that corner looking strong! Never skip out on your responsibilities; stay in there and fight, regardless of the odds. These standards give you depth of character; they make you a real person—a contender."*

Although right now she felt a tremendous need to get far away from the studio and Jason Banning, and yearned to escape, Corey realized that she mustn't follow that urge. With the light of a new day she recognized the necessity of facing the real world and all its problems.

Not only was her career at stake, but also she must prove to her enemy *and* to herself that she had the fortitude to go on the with the project she had begun and go on with her life. She must be strong for Cappy.

Cappy! She hadn't even thought of him! How *could* she be so thoughtless and self-centered? She'd been so wrapped up in her own pain and disappointment that she had completely forgotten about the friend who was so dear to her. He had been her confidant, had given her guidance. How utterly selfish she had been!

After all, Cappy was also a loser in this fiasco. He, too, had lost his savings and the part-ownership of the studio. He needed her friendship and moral support. She and Cappy had come through a lot together, and this would be no exception.

With this decision and the determination to follow her father's advice, Corey promptly retrieved the telephone receiver from its drawer and dialed Cappy's number.

She heard the distant ringing of the telephone and, as it continued to ring, began to wonder where he could be. Finally Corey was about to hang up when she heard Cappy's breathless answer.

"Cappy?"

"'Fraid so," he returned, then added, "Damn! I left the water running in the shower! Hold on a minute, will you?" He was gone before she could reply. After a brief wait Cappy was back on the line. "Corey. Are you all right?"

"I'm fine!"

"You sure?" Cappy pressed.

"Oh, Cappy, I'm so sorry. I've acted so irresponsibly!" Corey told him in a rush, the words tumbling out. "I should have been stronger. And I should have thought about you, not just about myself. I was so selfish! Oh, Cappy, what you must think of me. What kind of friend am I? You've always been there for me, and I—"

"Whoa!" Cappy broke in. "I understand, honey; it was a real blow. Jason should have...he could have prepared you. Well, he could have handled it differently, more tactfully." He paused briefly, then went on, "Well, no matter how he told you, it would have been a shock. I'd already learned about it, and *I* should have broken it to you, but I just didn't know how. You've gone through so much, and I guess I just wanted to protect you."

"But you did try, Cappy dear. I wouldn't listen, remember? Cappy, can't we fight this? Isn't there anything we can do?" she asked hopefully.

"Nothing!" he replied without hesitation. "I've seen the papers, Corey, and I've talked to the lawyers, and they explained the whole situation in detail. Matt knew what he was doing when he accepted the loan from Jason. You have to understand, Banning is as good a businessman as there is. After his father's death, he took over the family business and made it what it is today."

"I'll *never* accept what Jason Banning has done," Corey began angrily. "I've never in my life hated anyone, Cappy, but I hate that man!"

"Your hatred and bitterness is unwarranted, Corey."

"Is it?" she countered hotly. "I—"

"You're hurt and you're angry," Cappy broke in. You're angry at Matt for taking his own life and not anding up to his problems. You're angry at yourself—at fe. Jason just happens to be an easy target, Corey, and ou're not being fair."

When Corey remained silent, Cappy felt that he was per-aps getting through to her and went on, quietly. "You have) demonstrate that you are a responsible adult—one who ollows through with her commitments. Prove yourself. fter all, you're the daughter of Griff and Livia Kelton, and vo finer people never lived. Their daughter will be a credit) them, I know it."

There was complete silence at the other end of the line for n interminable moment, then Cappy heard a soft sigh fol-owed by Corey's subdued voice. "I'll see you on the set. .nd, Cappy? Thanks!"

Corey pulled into her parking space and sat motionless ehind the wheel. Her brown eyes took in the sight of the w-slung streamlined sports car that occupied the space ext to her. The sun shone down upon its highly polished .rface, its rich silver-gray glistening.

The car was elegant, sexy and handsome, just like its wner. She'd have to say one thing for Jason Banning: he ad class as well as expensive tastes.

She smiled unknowingly as her thoughts drifted back to ae first time she met Jason. She would never forget that day s long as she lived. It was as clear in her memory as if it had appened only yesterday....

Corey had been late for an appointment with her father ecause her acting class had run over. She'd raced into the arking lot, careening into what she thought to be an empty pace. She hadn't seen the low sports car that occupied the pace.

There was a loud, sickening crunch, and Corey was thrown backward as she rammed into the parked car. In dismay she stared wide-eyed at the very new, very expensive Mercedes, which still bore the price sticker on the window. She groaned, turned off the engine and stepped slowly from the car.

When she saw the damage, she cursed softly. Her father would kill her! Not to mention the unknown owner of the car. Red paint bled with light blue where the two cars fused.

A tall, lithe figure sprang from the car, and with a quick stride the man approached her. Corey's breath caught in her throat when she saw him—not so much because of the anger on his face but because of his arresting handsomeness. In all her sixteen years she had never seen a man as handsome. She knew who he was. She had seen his picture in the papers and in movie magazines, had seen him both on television and the screen. Jason Banning was the heartthrob of women, young and old. But in the flesh the man was devastating!

His face was darkly flushed beneath his tanned skin, and his chest rose and fell rapidly. He said nothing as his darkened green eyes glanced from Corey to the dent in his car and back again. He towered over her like some avenging god about to send a deadly lightning bolt down upon both her and her car.

Dumbfounded, Corey stared at the man. Willing her teeth to release the painful clench they held on her lower lip, she attempted to swallow the lump that had lodged in her throat.

Suddenly Jason spoke, his voice a husky sound that sent a warm sensation cascading down her spine to her toes. His green eyes held her motionless, their emerald brilliance almost blinding.

"One, you intended to do damage to my car. Two, you didn't see it. Or, three, you weren't watching where you were going," he enumerated, counting out the options on his strong, tanned fingers.

He was dead right on the last two counts, but she wasn't about to admit it, so she lied. Remembering that a strong offense is the best defense, Corey found her voice and snapped, "None of the above, sir! My—my brakes went out!" When she saw him crook one dark eyebrow disbelievingly, she took a deep breath and rushed on. "When I saw you, it was too late. I tried to stop but, well—" She broke off and pointed to the converged fenders. "I didn't," she concluded simply.

Banning stood for a moment, his gaze leisurely traveling over her as he slowly shook his dark head.

Corey became increasingly uncomfortable under his intense scrutiny. The expression on his face told her that he didn't believe her, and she bristled that he could see through her hastily improvised excuse.

"Well, if you don't believe me, then that's just too bad!" She glared at him, her hands on her trim waist, her voice sounding shrill and a little frightened.

"Who are you?" he asked quietly, his tone shocking her with its gentleness. Concern shone in his eyes.

"What?"

"Your name, sweetheart. You do have one, don't you?" he drawled lazily, the throaty sound causing her pulse to quicken.

"Of course I do," she returned spiritedly, though somewhat shaken by the soft timbre of his voice. "It's Corey."

"Corey, what?"

"Kelton. Corey Kelton."

"Griff Kelton's daughter." It wasn't a question. Jason leaned down from his towering six-foot-two height and braced his hands on top of the car hood, his green gaze holding hers. "Damn," he whispered, the word so soft she almost didn't hear it. "You're all grown-up, I see." He spoke louder now, and with undisguised interest.

Corey became even more uncomfortable under his searching gaze. "Mr. Banning, I—" she began.

"You know who I am?" he broke in, his green eyes dancing merrily and smiling that heart-stopping smile. His low, husky chuckle sent a warm flush over her, and an odd, unnamed emotion stirred deep within her.

"Everyone knows who you are," Corey told him somewhat haughtily.

"I'm impressed," Jason stated, leaning casually against the car, his stance dangerously sensuous.

Once again his gaze ran over Corey with leisure, in frank male admiration. His view was unobstructed, and he took his time, noting her small but shapely form clad in a blue-and-white tank top and matching jogging shorts. His eyes took in the firm high breasts and flat stomach and drifted downward, settling on the delicious curve of her hips before moving on to long, tanned legs. Then he looked back at her flushed face, his gaze resting on her soft lips.

"Yes, very impressed," he murmured.

"Because I know who you are?" Corey asked bluntly, a little tremor running through her at the look he was giving her.

"No. Impressed with Griff's daughter," he replied matter-of-factly.

Corey's heart slammed against her breast, and she could hardly breathe. The collision and the damage to his new car seemed to be forgotten as they stared at each other, a silent message passing between them.

With an effort Corey dragged her mind back to the problem at hand. "Uh, Mr. Banning—"

"Jason."

"Mr. Banning, about your car..." The words trailed away, her voice sounding strained to her own ears. "If you'll

ust let my father know what the damage is, I'll reimburse—"

"Why, I wouldn't think of it, darlin'," Jason broke in, his
one low and seductive, his green eyes burning into hers.
'I'll take care of the damage, sweetheart; you take care of
our faulty brakes."

Corey hadn't been aware that he had moved until she realized that Jason was standing just inches away, his hand
cupping her chin, his thumb tracing her lower lip.

"Next time you might not be so lucky, and I wouldn't
want any damage done to that lovely body of yours," he
breathed. His mouth came down upon hers with maddening softness, and he kissed her with aching tenderness.
Corey whimpered, and Jason groaned with feeling and
broke the kiss but didn't move away from her.

"How old are you, Corey?" he whispered against her
lips.

"S-sixteen," she answered weakly, her body trembling.

"God, what a shame," Jason muttered and set her from
him.

With those words he stepped around Corey, slid into her
car and started the engine. He put the gears in reverse and
backed slowly, breaking contact with his own vehicle, and
then pulled into an empty parking space a few cars over.

Jason strode back to where Corey stood and, with a
flourish, handed her the keys to her car. Then he stepped to
his own automobile, slipped behind the wheel and turned on
the ignition.

The quiet purr of the engine seemed unusually loud to
Corey's ears as she watched Jason pull out of the parking
place. She wondered fleetingly if she'd ever see again this
uncommonly good-looking, totally unpredictable man.

The Mercedes moved slowly forward, then stopped. Jason's dark gaze lingered on her for a brief moment, and he
smiled and shook his head, then drove out of the lot.

Corey stood there for an endless moment, her emotions in an uproar.

For days she mentally relived everything that had happened, heard again every word that had been spoken. No matter how many times she replayed it in her mind, it just didn't make sense. Jason had flung himself from his battered car like a raging bull, cursing, his face furious, then suddenly he had become calm and solicitous of her, all in a matter of seconds.

His anger had been real enough but had subsided to the degree that he had been cool and controlled and, to her surprise, had seemed openly interested in her as a woman. Until she had told him her age.

Jason never told her father about the accident and neither did she. But she had never seen Jason again. He'd been cast as the leading man in a movie to be filmed in Mexico and had left shortly after their encounter. She had asked many questions about the handsome star, learning that both her mother and father held Jason Banning in high regard as a person as well as an actor.

So through her teenage years, Jason Banning had been Corey's secret: his kiss, his words had lived in her heart, in her dreams. He had been her dream lover, and she had believed herself in love with him. She had compared him with the boys she dated, and none had ever measured up to him, of course.

Even into her adult years Corey had made the same comparison with every man she dated. She had never forgotten Jason Banning. . . .

But *now* she knew what kind of man he really was! He had shattered her treasured image of him and showed his true self, a side of Jason Banning that no one else knew about. She hated him!

A tap on the car window startled Corey. She turned to see Ken James, the security guard for the studio, and rolled down the window.

"You okay, Miss Kelton?" he asked with concern.

"Hi, Ken. Yes, I'm okay." She smiled brightly, reassuring him.

"Well, I saw you drive in, but when you took so long... Well, I just wanted to make sure."

"I'm afraid you caught me daydreaming," she told him as she opened the door to get out. Reaching in the back seat, she retrieved her briefcase and tote bag. "Thank you for your concern, Ken."

"Oh, sure, Miss Kelton," he beamed and stood a little straighter, throwing back his slim shoulders. "I've been here at Fielder for a long time. Why, I've seen you grow up, miss," Ken told her proudly. "I care about you."

Corey turned her warm brown eyes to the old man and placed her hand on his bony arm. "And you mean a great deal to me. Thank you for caring, Ken. It's good to know that someone cares."

"Yes, miss, and I sure do."

Four

Well, well, well! I see you decided to return to work.'' The sarcastic voice of Jason Banning carried along the hallway as he strode leisurely toward Corey. "Thought better of the brash words you spouted so bravely yesterday?"

Corey stopped with her hand on the doorknob of her dressing room. Having no desire to see the loathsome Jason, she refused to turn around and made to enter the room. But his strong arm swept out, barring her way, and she took a step backward to avoid his touch.

Jason moved to lean casually against the doorframe, a lazy smile playing about his sensuous lips. His green eyes sparked with surprise and pleasure at the sight of Corey. He had seen the banked fires in the depths of her tawny eyes, had hoped that she would be a fighter. And he secretly admired her for having sustained such an emotional blow and having the courage and stamina to bounce back, apparently undaunted.

"Cappy assured me that you'd be back," Jason told her with a chuckle. "I must admit that I'm a bit surprised, sweetheart, especially after yesterday's violent reaction to our heated exchange."

Corey drew a deep, ragged breath and exhaled slowly before attempting a reply to his comment. Focusing her attention on a button on his shirt rather than meeting Jason's eyes, she managed a curt retort. "If you'll get out of my way, Mr. Banning, I'll be able to get ready for the day's shooting. As you so pointedly reminded me, the longer it takes to do this film, the more time and money it costs this company. And far be it from me to run up production costs!"

Corey's words were intensely irritating to Jason, yet he knew he had asked for them. Why am I goading her, he wondered fleetingly, when I should be attempting to befriend her? But before he could placate her, she spoke again.

"Also, as you were so pleased to inform me, you now own Fielder Studios *and* my contract. I'm obligated to complete this film, and I'll do so, but there's nothing in my contract to the effect that I have to make polite conversation or be social with you. Future scripts and contractual agreements will be handled and negotiated by Fielder Studios due to the fact that there are two remaining years before my contract expires and I'm free of you."

Her words had been spoken in a very brisk, businesslike manner but with an undertone of bitterness. Corey raised her head and pinned Jason with her piercing golden-brown eyes and concluded, "Now we both know where I stand. And I know where *you* stand—in my way! So move *out* of the way, Mr. Banning!"

She took a purposeful step forward, fully expecting him to move, but he stood his ground, and she walked right into Jason's steely arm with which once again he barred her way.

Glancing quickly up at him, Corey found his smoldering emerald stare burning into her.

"I don't take kindly to being ordered about, Corey," he said with an edge of anger. "You'll do well to remember that."

There was a long, uncomfortable silence while their gazes locked and each of them waited for the other to make a move.

"If you would perhaps ask nicely," Jason suggested softly, a slight huskiness in his voice.

Corey stood her ground, her eyes flashing with golden fire, her lips pressed in a thin line of determination, even though her body was trembling with anger and an unnamed emotion.

"Corey..." Jason sighed with feeling as he moved from the door and reached out to touch her flushed cheek.

Corey jumped as if she had been burned. She slipped past him into the dressing room and attempted to close the door. But Jason's arm shot out, the weight of his outstretched hand stopping the door just short of the latch.

"Just leave me alone!" she cried desperately.

Again she tried to push the door shut. Realizing that he had no intention of allowing her to close the door in his face, Corey shrugged indifferently and turned her back on him. As she crossed the room, she heard the door close softly. She lifted her eyes to the mirror and met his cool green gaze.

"We need to talk, Corey."

"I have *nothing* to say to you," she returned breathlessly. "And I don't want to hear anything you have to say." Her voice broke, and a small, choking sounded rattled in her throat. "Please, Jason," she said, her tone weary, her tawny eyes pleading. "Please, just go away and leave me alone."

"I'll go, Corey, after I say what I came to say," he countered.

She watched as he walked nearer, steeled herself for his touch and, conversely, was oddly disappointed when he made no attempt to do so. Rather, he stood with his hands shoved into his pockets, his gaze roaming over her in his usual disturbing manner.

"I know it was a shock when you found out I own the studio. That something you believed to be yours had been taken away from you. I should have handled it differently. But I didn't, and there's no changing that," Jason explained. "I can only apologize for my thoughtlessness," he added, with a new gentleness in his voice.

His apology was met with cold silence, neither accepted nor rejected, and after a long moment Jason continued speaking. "I want to explain about Matt Fielder, about the studio and my takeover."

"I don't want to hear any of your lies, Jason Banning!" Corey turned on him with fury. "You stole this studio from Cappy and me."

"I stole nothing from either of you," Jason said flatly, controlling his own rising temper. "Matt accepted a loan from Banning Productions. The business dealings between us were legal and binding."

"Legal...binding! What is it with you, Banning? Do you think that a piece of paper, drawn up by *your* lawyers, makes your being a thief *legal*?" she cried. "I don't know how you managed it. God, I wish I did, for it would make it easier to fight you, because fight you I will! If it takes the rest of my life and every damned cent I have, I'll fight your claim to Fielder Studios!"

"You'll lose," Jason stated bluntly and without hesitation.

"That remains to be seen," Corey countered hotly. "Cappy—"

"Will do nothing!" he broke in. "Unlike you, he has accepted the truth of this matter. Cappy realizes that Matt defaulted on our agreement weeks before he killed himself. Dammit, Corey, I gave the man a chance!''

"Like hell you did!" she spat. "Matt told me how you helped him. He begged for your help, only to have you laugh in his face. And you laughed at what you called our 'feeble attempt' to save the studio with our 'puny' savings. Well, that money, *our* 'puny' savings that Cappy and I gave Matt—that money saved Fielder Studios!''

"My God, Corey, do you really believe that? Do you have any idea just how deeply in debt Matt really was? The fifteen thousand that you and Cappy scraped up, between you, didn't make a dent in what he owed. It took another seventy-five thousand to bail him out!''

"You're a liar!" Corey screamed, striking out at Jason in blind fury. "You're a liar, a thief, a murderer! Oh, I hate you! Hate you!''

Her flailing fists ceased their violent attack, and Corey dropped her limp hands to her sides. Slowly she turned away from Jason, her bright head bowed and her slim shoulders drooping in defeat. Her body shook with uncontrollable shudders while tears continued to rain unchecked.

"Oh, Corey," Jason murmured feelingly.

He covered the short distance between them and gently led the unresisting Corey to the nearby sofa. Lowering himself to the cushions, he pulled her into his embrace and tenderly held her while heartrending sobs tore from her slight body, sobs that tore at his own heart.

Her crying lessened and finally subsided, but when Corey stirred in his arms and made to move away, Jason tightened his hold, pressing her closer against his broad chest, unwilling to relinquish the embrace. His lips brushed her temple, and he breathed her name into the softness of her hair.

Emotionally spent, Corey lay heavily against him, her body responding to the warmth of him. Jason's gentleness erased, for the moment, all the enmity and bitterness she felt toward him. Strangely, she felt secure in the arms of the man she despised and was surprised at his tenderness. This was yet another side to Jason Banning that she hadn't seen before.

Corey became aware of the deep, quiet timbre of Jason's voice, yet her thoughts occupied her mind to such a degree that she hadn't been concentrating on his words. Slowly they began to register.

"... and Matt used you," he was saying bluntly. "It was common knowledge, Corey, but your friends were trying to protect you from the truth. The money you and Cappy gave to salvage the studios was thrown away on liquor and gambling. It's time someone told you. The sooner you realize this fact, the better for you."

His words cut deeply, causing a sharp, searing pain to rip unmercifully through Corey. Lies! Oh, dear God, what was Jason trying to do to her? Was he so unfeeling, so heartless? Matt was unable to come to his own defense, but she was still here, and she could most assuredly make him retract his absurd accusations.

With frenzied haste Corey struggled out of Jason's arms. "How could you?" she stormed, springing to her feet, her eyes fired with fury. *"How dare you!"* Corey stood over him, anger, confusion and pain washing over her in wave after wave. "I won't listen to any more of your lies!"

Whirling around, she stomped across the room and jerked the door open, holding it wide. "Get out, Mr. Banning!" she gritted. "Just get out!" The last was said almost in a whisper.

Jason stared at her for a moment, shook his head in disbelief and stood from the sofa. He ran his fingers through his hair, and a muscle jerked along his jawline. Then he strode to the door but stopped short.

"You don't want to hear the truth," he informed Corey softly. "But the truth is something we *all* must face, sooner or later, whether we want to or not. Life isn't always the way we want it to be, Corey. People aren't always what we want them to be, or what we believe them to be. You may not want to hear this, but the *truth* is that Matt Fielder was a compulsive gambler and drinker.

"Why do you think he was in such a financial mess? Why do you think no one was willing to take a chance on him?" Jason persisted, trying to bring home some truths, to make her see and understand fact. "I'll tell you why. He was untrustworthy and unreliable. That much you should realize after what he did to you and Cappy and Fielder Studios! He was a weak man, sweetheart. Everyone else knows it, and you may as well know it, too. Wake up, Corey, face the bald truth, for God's sake!"

With those words Jason stalked out, slamming the door behind him and leaving a very shaken Corey in his wake.

On unsteady legs Corey walked across the room and sank into the chair before her makeup mirror, fighting back the tears. With shaking hands she picked up a jar of makeup and automatically began to apply it to her pale face, her hands making short, jerky movements. Only by tremendous effort did she choke back the tears.

She hated Jason for painting such an ugly picture of Matt. She would never forgive him for his cruel words, his arrogance, nor for the hurt he was causing her. Nor would she *ever* forgive him for taking what rightfully belonged to her and Cappy.

Jason had said Matt was untrustworthy, unreliable and that due to these flaws she and Cappy had been used, their money thrown away because of Matt's weakness for gambling and liquor. Matt, a weak man?

As Corey sat before the mirror, staring unseeingly into its depths, her mind began to remember things that her heart had chosen to forget and to ignore. She was forced to look back, to see, to hear, to acknowledge. She remembered the hushed whispers she had overheard at various times that had quieted when she arrived, the exchange of knowing looks, concern and even pity.

She remembered the times at parties when she would hear Matt's name, then hear the sibilant sound of *shh* followed by an embarrassed silence. And yet on other occasions, at the studio, as she neared the set she would sometimes hear the buzz of conversation. Then someone would whisper loudly, "Here comes Corey," and immediately there were furtive glances her way, some a bit guilty, and awkward silence.

They knew! Oh, God, they *all* knew. *Everybody* knew but Corey Kelton. She had been a fool! Suddenly so many pieces of the puzzle began to fall into place, and, although she didn't want to see Matt as a loser, he must have been. Although she didn't want to believe Jason's words, the truth of them were hitting home.

Corey closed her eyes tightly and in her mind's eye saw Cappy as he had tried unsuccessfully to tell her things she refused to hear. She recalled Jason's efforts to explain those same things. The most amazing part of it all was that now, as the words of both men came back to her, Corey could very plainly hear the absolute ring of truth in the voices of both, could see their eyes, unclouded by lies or deceit.

How could she have been so blind? How could she have been so stupid? How could she have been so negative that she wouldn't at least show them the courtesy of hearing them out? She could always have told them she didn't believe them, *after* she had had the decency to listen to what they had to say.

Now she saw Matt as someone she truly hadn't known. He'd been a stranger and, obviously, something of a louse. No longer could she refuse to see what everyone else had seen, refuse to listen to what everybody else had heard, refuse to believe what everyone else already knew.

"Oh, Matt, why?" she cried brokenly. "You were all I had left! I loved you, trusted you, believed in you. Damn you, Matt, you were my strength!" She laughed bitterly. "Strength? God, what a joke! What a fool I was—*I am!*" she amended shrilly, throwing the makeup bottle at the mirror with all her might. "What a colossal fool," she whispered, her blurred gaze resting on the tan liquid that slowly trailed down the broken mirror in uneven lengths, the shattered glass radiating in weblike cracks from the center.

"Corey?"

The concerned voice of Cappy penetrated her thoughts and she turned to see him in the doorway, his face pale and drawn, his light blue eyes showing worry and pain.

"Oh, Cappy," Corey cried in despair, burying her face in her shaking hands. "Why did this have to happen? How could Matt do this to us?"

"Questions I've asked myself a hundred times, honey," Cappy told her, seating himself in the chair next to her. "Matt had changed, Corey. We both knew something was wrong, and we tried to help. He wouldn't let us."

"But the money! He took our money, he—"

"That wasn't the kind of help he needed from us. He needed our love, our strength, but when it was offered, freely given, well, it just wasn't enough. He was too far gone, too deep in his personal hell, the sickness of his weakness, his habits," he told her honestly. "I knew how hard you would take all this.

"I'm sorry, honey, I tried to tell you, but I—I just couldn't. I was still trying to protect you. I didn't want to cause you more pain, and I didn't want to be the one to destroy your love for Matt, and your image of him. It was my place to tell you: Jason made me see that. I should have told you before Jason did."

"Matt had no right, Cappy. He had no right to do this! He owed both of us. Not because of the money, but because of our faith, our support, our love," Corey reasoned in a perplexed tone.

"You're hurting, Corey. We both are," Cappy told her soothingly, and placed a fatherly arm gently around her young shoulders. "It'll take time to heal the wounds we've suffered. Time!" Then, in his usual optimistic manner, he chuckled and added, "And that's about all we've got left out of all this. So we should heal beautifully!"

"Oh, Cappy!" Corey cried, burrowing her head into his shoulder. "What would I do if I didn't have you?"

"Well, that's one thing you'll never have to find out!" he promised her solemnly. Then, on a more cheerful note, he said "Now, chin up! You and me, we're survivors! So wipe the tears from those lovely eyes and pull yourself together. We've got things to do and worlds to conquer!"

Five

——

And, hold...two...three...four. That's a wrap! Okay, everybody, 6:00 a.m. call tomorrow!''

Cappy's voice resounded across the set, calling the long day of shooting to an end. The cameras ground to a halt, the bright lights were turned down, and immediately an unintelligible rumble of voices burst out to roll across the large room. Cast and crew began moving gingerly about, stretching their weary bodies.

It had been another long, tiring day, one of several in which they had attempted to get the production schedule back on target. Much valuable time had been lost during the tragedy of Matt's death, and they had worked hard to make up the lost time.

Knowing that tomorrow would be another long workday, which, as Cappy had just informed them, would begin early, the cast dispersed rapidly. Workmen began preparing the set for the next day's shooting.

Corey was slumped in the chair where the last scene had left her, too weary to pull her body up. Her legs felt too weak to propel her across the stage, down the hall to her dressing room. If it were left up to her, she wouldn't budge an inch, but would sit there until tomorrow when everyone else showed up for work. The idea appealed to her.

Finally, with a groan, Corey heaved herself up and stood on trembling legs. She drew a ragged breath and exhaled it through her teeth. Whisking a wayward curl from her brow, she massaged her temples with her fingertips, wishing that the painful throbbing of her headache would subside.

God, but she was tired! No, tired wasn't a strong enough word for what she felt. Ten days of 6:00 a.m. calls and working sometimes until midnight or after. She had been making her way home to shower and fall into bed, completely fatigued, hoping for an uninterrupted four or five hours' of sleep—if, indeed, sleep would come to her at all. Many nights she had lain sleepless for the greater portion of the time, falling into exhausted slumber for what seemed like mere minutes before having to get up for the day.

Corey had long since realized that her body had begun to rebel against the abuse it was taking, yet she had refused to listen to its protests, or heed its warnings. She had stubbornly pushed herself to go on and on, her reasoning being that the sooner she was finished with this project the sooner she would be away from Jason Banning.

After *this* film, she determined grimly, she wouldn't have to deal with the man. As an actress contracted to Fielder Studios—soon to be renamed Banning Productions, Incorporated—she thought bitterly, any further dealings would be handled over the telephone or through the studio's agency. Should it become necessary for personal negotiations . . . well, she'd cross that bridge when she came to it.

All this passed through Corey's mind as she walked stiffly toward her dressing room, forcing one foot to follow the other. Her body was crying out for rest, and once again, she was deliberately ignoring it.

Once in the small room, Corey applied a generous amount of cold cream and mechanically wiped off the stage makeup. Tiredly she shed her costume and pulled on a pair of jeans and an oversize jersey. Glimpsing her reflection in the mirror, she gasped, then walked slowly toward the glass to peer closely.

"Oh, my God," she breathed in dismay, touching her pale face with shaking fingers as she studied the woman staring back at her, arrested by the image she saw. "What are you doing to yourself?"

Corey's dull eyes drifted over her thinning frame. The jeans that had once fit so snugly were showing signs of being too large. They hung low on hips that threatened to lose the sexy curve they normally boasted, and drooped noticeably in the rear. The waistband had room to spare.

Raising her gaze, Corey saw that her eyes seemed to stare out of deep-set sockets. God! What a sight, she thought, appalled at the apparition in the looking-glass.

No wonder Cappy had looked so worried when he told her she wasn't looking well. No wonder that her fellow workers glanced at her, then looked quickly away, but not before she had seen their concern. No wonder that Jason Banning scowled at her so often and had whispered once "You look awful, kid" during a scene in today's shooting when he seated her and bowed low over her. His whispered words had caused to her bristle, and she shot him a heated look, pulled free of his hold and continued her lines.

Now, despite her extreme exhaustion, her tired brain brought to her memory the fact that she had rested little, eaten less, and had scarcely noticed her body for days. She had only seen her reflection as she hurriedly applied stage makeup and had paid no attention to the fact that her face had thinned and her cheeks had deep hollows in them.

"You won't win any beauty contests looking like this, Kelton!" she said frankly as she stuffed her tote bag with makeup, a pair of shoes and a few miscellaneous items. With one last glance at herself, she informed the mirrored image, "You look like some zombie out of a bad horror movie!"

Slinging the large canvas bag over her shoulder, Corey left her dressing room and crossed the near-deserted studio. Wearily she made her way along the outer hallway that led to the exit and, eventually, to the parking lot, lost in thought and wondering that the almighty Jason Banning had allowed her to remain in the film looking the way she did. Of course, her stage wardrobe for this movie was all period costumes that hid her thin body. And she remembered that Cappy had frequently asked the makeup artist to add extra makeup and touches to her face. Now she knew why!

"Corey!"

The deep resonance of Jason's voice startled her, and Corey turned to see him lounging against the frame in an open doorway near the end of the hall, apparently for the express purpose of intercepting her.

"I was just leaving, Mr. Ban—"

"I want to talk with you, Corey," Jason cut in, waving his hand toward his office.

"Look, I'm tired, I want to go home. I-I don't want to talk to you," she told him honestly, although somewhat shakily, and turned to leave.

"I said I wanted to talk with you!" he bit out, pushing his lithe body from the door. He walked to her, grasped her upper arms with his steely grip and steered her back down the hall and into the office.

"Sit!" he barked, pointing to a nearby chair.

"I'll stand."

"Don't push me, Corey; you wouldn't like the consequences." His dark green eyes pinned her with their blatant anger. "So sit!"

She made no move to do so, only tilted her chin in defiance. Her tawny eyes flashed with rebellion.

"Don't fight with me, Corey. I'm much better at it than you are, and I'm afraid you'd only endanger yourself."

Corey saw the truth of his statement and bit her lower lip in an effort to still the heated words she wanted to throw at him. Slowly she sank to the edge of the chair and stared unblinkingly at Jason, her own anger reflected in her stormy eyes. She may not be able to win this round, but there would undoubtedly be another, and she was determined to be prepared for it! She may have to succumb to his tactics, but she would make no secret of her dislike for the man and his high-handed treatment of her.

She watched in impatient silence as Jason crossed the room to settle himself on the corner of his desk. Corey couldn't help staring and thirstily drank in the sight of his perfectly proportioned body. She drew a quick breath, her heart fluttering uncomfortably, and shifted uneasily in her chair.

Although it made her furious to admit it, the simple truth was that Jason Banning was as sexy as all get out! The man fairly oozed sensuality. His every move seemed a blatant enjoyment of sensual pleasure and he radiated sexuality and self-assurance.

Authority was ever present in his voice, his stance, in the keen eyes that forever held a hint of raw passion within their emerald depths. His expression, when not angry, was indifferently curious, mysterious and exciting. Overwhelmingly attractive, Jason was fully aware of the fact.

Corey felt herself hopelessly drawn to him and was instantly repulsed. Why was she so weak when it came to Jason? Why did he affect her, no matter how much she de-

ied the attraction? No matter how desperately she fought
is magnetism?

"I'm concerned about you, Corey."

Jason's voice roused her from her mesmerized state, and
with a pounding heart, she started guiltily.

"Your concern is touching but unnecessary," she replied
bluntly, her gaze steadily on him. "Now, if you don't mind,
'm going home."

Corey made to rise, but Jason's hands gripped her shoulders like a steel vise, and he thrust her back into the chair
none too gently. Only by sheer self-control did she prevent
herself from crying out.

"I *do* mind!" he ground out between clenched teeth,
standing threateningly over her. "*Everything* about you
concerns me, Corey, therefore I make it my business. You
have an obligation, not only to me, this studio, and this
project, but to yourself! And you're doing a godawful job
of it," he reproached her scathingly.

As Corey sat stonily silent, Jason turned and walked a few
paces away, then retraced his steps to again stand before her.

"You're looking pretty worn-out," he said on a quieter
note. "And, if I'm not mistaken, you've lost weight."

He made it sound like a crime, Corey thought indignantly, resenting his interference in such a personal problem.

"If I'm looking worn-out, Mr. Banning, it is because I
am!" she returned icily. "You, as well as I, know that the
hours we've been putting in have been anything but short.
I'm working, just as everyone else, to make up the lost time
and get this film back on schedule.

"And if I'm losing weight," Corey continued spiritedly,
"it's none of your damned business!" She tossed her head
scornfully.

"It *is* my business!" Jason shot back. "I want to see this
film wrapped up and, from where I stand, it looks as if you

might conk out on us before it's done. Dammit, Corey, have you looked at yourself recently? I mean *really* looked at yourself? There's no nice way of saying it: to be brutally blunt, you look like hell."

"Thank you," she said unemotionally.

"Damn you, woman!" Jason roared, raising his fists in the air in frustration. His face flushed an angry red, a vein throbbed at his temple, and tension vibrated between them.

"Why are you forever fighting me? Why?" he questioned. "Do you get some kind of sadistic thrill from prodding me? One way or another, you seem determined to try my patience. What is it with you?" he demanded with feeling. "I am truly worried about you. Can't you see that?"

"Oh, I can see!" Corey shot back, coming to her feet. She stood inches from him, facing him with her anger. "You're worried that your precious movie might be interrupted, or even postponed. You're worried about production costs! You're worried that this film might never be finished! That's what you're worried about, Jason Banning! *They* mean something to you. Don't think me a fool. Your so-called concern is because I, the actress in a crucial role, may become ill and not be able to carry on. Mr. Banning, you're all heart, aren't you?

"Well, let me set your mind at ease. I'll be right here every hour of every day of shooting. I would never allow something as trivial as becoming ill to stand in the way of this film. I've never wanted anything more in my life than to finish this project. Because when it's over, I'll be rid of the likes of you. I won't have to endure your touch, be held or kissed by you, won't have to speak to you, won't even have to look at you. So rest assured, Banning, your damned movie won't be endangered by me!" Corey spat with venom. "I'll be here until the last scene is played and Cappy says 'and, hold, two, three, four...that's a wrap!' " she intoned in her best imitation of the director's voice.

"To hell with the movie!" Jason bit out through clenched teeth. Gripping her arms, he shook her from utter frustration. "I'm worried about you, Corey. *You!*"

"Oh, that is rich, Banning. Really rich." She laughed without humor. "I've always known you were a good actor, but you've really outdone yourself on this performance. Too bad I'm your only audience, you might—"

"Shut up, Corey!" The words were spoken in a velvety soft tone but with the cut of steel. Jason's gaze burned into her, suppressed fury sparking in the emerald depths of his eyes. "Damn you, Corey. Damn you!" he breathed raggedly. Realizing he still held her in his strong grip, he released his hold and moved away from her.

Jason walked to the window and stood looking out, clenching and unclenching his fists at his sides, his jaw set tightly, his body rigid.

Corey could hear his labored breath, see his tremendous struggle to rein in his temper and gain control. To her horror, she felt for Jason and, without warning, compassion twisted like a living thing in her breast.

"Jason, I—" Corey began uneasily, but her words were drowned by those of Jason.

"You deliberately do anything and everything you can to anger me. You challenge everything I say, oppose everything I do. You go to great lengths to hurt, and choose your words carefully in order to inflict the deepest, most painful wounds," he said flatly, shaking his head in bewilderment.

Slowly Jason turned to face Corey, fixing her with his open gaze.

She was taken aback by the raw emotion mirrored there. Had she truly been so cruel? Had her words of hurt and anger so wounded him? Was there more to this man than she had seen? After all, she had refused to see so much. Was there depth to Jason—kindness, gentleness, loving? Her thoughts rushed forward, crowding her mind.

"Have you total disregard for your health? Would you go so far as to literally kill yourself from neglect, just to—" His words broke off, and he drew in his breath sharply at the sight of Corey's stony stare, her expression devoid of any emotion. "My God!" Jason breathed. "I believe you would!"

He stared at her in perplexity for a long moment, then walked blindly around the desk and sank wearily into the leather chair. Leaning his dark head against the headrest, he closed his eyes and covered his face with both hands. After a moment he dropped his hands but remained where he was, his eyes still closed.

"I knew you hated me, Corey. But I had no idea of the magnitude of that hatred! Not until now." The words were quiet, and the tone was weary.

An uneasy silence gripped the room. Jason remained seated, unmoving and wordless, his eyes closed. He gave no indication of being aware of Corey's presence.

She stood, somewhat shaken, in the middle of the room. She, too, waited unmovingly and wordless, staring at Jason as the uncomfortable silence lengthened.

"Go home, Corey," he said heavily.

His voice held none of the usual ridicule or sarcasm, Corey thought. Rather it carried the sound of helplessness. Helplessness? Jason Banning, helpless? No, she was mistaken. He was many things, but not helpless. She must be imagining things because she was so tired.

She peered more closely at the object of her scrutiny. He, too, seemed tired, his features drawn, his mouth unsmiling. He looked kind of lost . . . alone.

Suddenly Corey felt the urge to gently stroke the frown from Jason's brow, to run a finger across the tight lips and see them relax. She actually took a step forward, then stopped, appalled at her thoughts. She stiffened with self-contempt and laughed inwardly at such rashness.

Taking a deep, unsteady breath, Corey retrieved her oversize bag, walked to the door and opened it. Before stepping through the doorway, she glanced over her shoulder to find Jason's dark gaze upon her. Their eyes met and held for the briefest moment before Corey walked out, closing the door behind her.

Jason stared at the closed door. He sat tensely, his nerves tightly strung, his senses whirling, his thoughts running rampant. The only noticeable movement of the man was the rise and fall of his chest, the occasional blink of his eyes.

He was astounded at Corey's interpretation of what he had said. Would he ever get through to her? Why had he felt it necessary to voice his concern for her? Had he actually believed that she would listen and understand? What was the use, anyway? he thought, for the moment mystified by the entire situation.

Why did he, Jason Banning, forever waste his time with Corey Kelton? His stomach tightened, and he groaned aloud, knowing the answer.

Love.

Corey had been a dangerous temptation to him for many years now. At sixteen the woman-child had intrigued him, stirred his desire with the promise of passion banked in the depths of her innocent eyes. She had been a beauty and had captured his heart. Although unaware of the fact, she still held it with an iron grip after all this time.

Jason's heart quickened as the vivid memory surged forward and turned back the time....

Jason had finished his meeting with Griff Kelton, had obtained his agreement to coproduce the film *Dark Waters* with Banning Productions. He had also managed to secure Livia Kelton in the starring role. He felt great! The world couldn't have been better for him, at that moment.

He was about to pull from his parking space when a small sports car careened around the car beside him and crashed into his car with a jolting blow.

"Damn!" the oath erupted loudly as Jason's temper flared.

For a moment he sat confusedly before opening his door to confront the imbecile who had senselessly rammed a parked car.

The stinging reprimand died on his lips as he was brought up abruptly by the vision of beauty standing uncertainly before him. Never, even in his wildest dreams, would he have thought to meet destiny head-on.

But there she stood. A tousled mess of lush, chestnut-colored hair caressed the loveliest face he'd ever seen. A perfect body was barely covered by a tank top and shorts, and her skin was a sun-kissed tan. He was mesmerized by the long, shapely legs. Tawny gold-flecked eyes held Jason spellbound and speechless.

She was a beauty! She took his breath away. All rational thought escaped him, and he could only concentrate on the young woman standing at arm's length away. In that moment she had captured his heart so completely that she was to hold it for an eternity.

Suddenly Jason found his voice and attempted to focus on the mishap and the damage to his new automobile. He had great difficulty in doing so; his car was the furthest thing from his mind.

When he learned her identity, he was pleased with the discovery. Due to the recent agreement between Jason Banning and the Keltons, he would have the opportunity to see her often.

As their conversation proceeded, Jason held himself in check, fighting the urge to reach out and touch Corey, to discover for himself if her skin was as smooth, as satiny, as it appeared. Her soft, heady scent beckoned him, and he was filled with a consuming need for her. Unable to suppress the desire to kiss her lips, taste their honeyed sweetness and touch her fire just once, his lips met hers in maddening tenderness.

When Corey whimpered softly, the sound caused Jason's emotions to soar. Passion flamed with intense heat, threatening to engulf him, and he knew with certainty that he would never be able to get enough of her.

"How old are you, Corey?" he whispered against her trembling lips.

And when she answered "sixteen," Jason thought he would surely die. "God, what a shame," he muttered, setting her from him. He stood looking down at her in shock.

Once in his car, he drove away from Fielder Studios and Corey Kelton as if the devil himself was in pursuit. Sixteen! How could a mere slip of a girl have such a devastating effect on him? An involuntary spasm shook him, and he felt his throat tighten. Jason had never wanted a woman with the fever in which he wanted Corey Kelton! Sixteen! Good Lord Almighty!

Touching his forefinger to his lips, the remembrance of their kiss sprang forth. Jason had kissed a young girl of sixteen, but it had been a woman who had returned his kiss, who had stirred his desire and fanned the fires of passion that burned within the man.

He would have to stay away from Corey and her sensual allure, Jason warned himself sternly. He had courted danger, and he would have to get far away, for the temptation was too powerful; he'd never have the strength to deny it.

Within a week's time Jason had signed for the lead in a movie being filmed on location in Mexico. Two weeks later he was thousands of miles away from Corey, yet she was still with him. "Out of sight, out of mind" as the saying went, yet the cliché proved to be a meaningless one. For the vivid memory of Corey Kelton was with Jason during his every waking moment and followed him into his dreams.

Just one month after his encounter with Griff and Livia's beautiful daughter, word was received that the couple had died suddenly and tragically. It had taken all the strength Jason could muster not to leave Mexico and go to Corey. His need to comfort her was overwhelming. He wanted nothing more than to hold her in his arms, to be there for her, to share her sorrow.

And the knowledge that he could not do so caused Jason unbearable pain. He had left his heart and soul with Corey and knew he would never be whole without her.

"You thought the years would change that, didn't you?" Jason asked himself now.

His voice rang hollowly in the emptiness of the room. Reaching into the back pocket of his denim jeans, he drew out his wallet and opened it. His gaze rested on the beautiful image of Corey.

"Will I ever have you? Will I ever know your love?" he whispered, running his thumb lovingly over the likeness. "So many years, my love. For so long I've loved you— wanted you."

Six

―――

Corey, honey, where in God's name are you?'' Cappy asked the empty room, his hands stuffed deep into his pockets as he paced the floor of Corey's dressing room, concern etched on his face.

It was a few minutes past eight, and Corey had yet to show for the day's shooting. Cappy had never known her to miss a shoot or to be overly late, for that matter. His attempts to reach her had failed, even though he had dialed her number repeatedly. Something had to be wrong!

The door opened, and Cappy whirled toward it expectantly, but saw that it was Jason who entered.

"Any word?" Jason questioned, his own face drawn.

"None," the other answered with a bewildered shake of his graying head. "This isn't like Corey." Cappy stated in a voice that was decidedly worried. "Not like her at all." He glanced at his watch for what must have been the hundredth time. "It's been over two hours! I tell you, Jason, something is definitely wrong!'' His voice was rough with emotion.

"Have you tried calling her?''

"Hell, yes!'' Cappy bristled with resentment. "Why would you think I haven't? Dammit, Jason, Corey means a great deal to me! Christ, she's like my own flesh and blood.''

"Cappy, I'm only trying to find a reason as to why she isn't here. You don't have to bite my head off,'' Jason returned, the deep undercurrent of concern belying the calmness of his words.

His own worry for Corey ate at him, and his stomach felt as if it were tied in knots. She had gone through so much in the past few weeks. She was confused, had suffered acute disappointment and was working too long hours. She was physically and mentally fatigued, and it was showing.

The signs were all there: her pallor; her loss of weight; her faltering and having trouble recalling her lines; her general apathy.

That was why he had tried to talk to her last night. But that had been a disaster! Hurtful words had been exchanged, nothing had been accomplished and she'd left with all the bitterness and hatred still coiled deep within her.

"Jason, you two didn't have words again?'' Cappy stared keenly at the younger man and immediately knew the answer. He ran his hands distractedly through his hair and groaned. "Is there no end to your battling? Can't you two call a truce, *something?*''

"Her hatred for me goes too deep, my friend.''

"There's a very thin line between hate and love, Jason.''

"'He quoted the cliché without conviction,''' Jason responded without humor. "That's tripe,'' he said bluntly.

"Maybe so, but true, nevertheless,'' Cappy countered. "Could whatever you said to her last night upset her enough for her to pull a stunt like this? Maybe you—''

"*Me!* Was it something *I* did, something *I* said? Has it ever occurred to anyone around here that it might have been Corey who upset me, that she may have done something or said something that hurt me?" Jason flung the words heatedly. "Oh, no! It's unthinkable, unheard of, that little Miss Kelton could be anything other than the victim."

Flinging the door open, Jason stalked from the room, fury choking him. "I'll find her, dammit, and when I *do*, I'm going to wring that pretty little neck of hers! I'll..." His last words floated back down the hallway, then trailed into nothingness.

It was evident that the younger man's worry about Corey was just as great and just as sincere as his own, Cappy thought, even though the other tried very hard not to show it and probably would never admit it.

Cappy watched Jason's retreat with a mixture of relief and apprehension—relief because he knew that something would be done to locate Corey, and apprehension because when Jason *did* find her, Cappy fervently hoped Corey would be all right and that the consolation would serve to assuage Jason's frustration and anger.

Somewhere in the corridors of her mind, Corey heard the ringing of the telephone. She had heard it in the far-off distance, time and time again, but her consciousness would not respond. Now the ringing was penetrating, and she rolled over, her hand outstretched, and fumbled for the receiver. A clatter, followed by a dull thud, let her know she had knocked something over in the process, but she managed to grip the instrument, lift it from its cradle and bring it to her ear.

"Hello," her sleep-drugged voice answered drowsily.

She scarcely heard the voice at the other end of the line, as she dozed again. The receiver slipped from her lax fingers to fall on the floor.

"Hello! Hello, Corey?" an urgent voice drifted upward, only to reach deaf ears.

"Dammit, Corey, answer me! Corey!" Jason slammed the phone down and headed out of his office, colliding with a startled Cappy in the hall. "Stand by, Cappy. I'll call you when I know something" was all he said and was out the door.

The low-slung sports car was whirled into the driveway of Regency House Condos where Corey lived, and Jason Banning leaped from the vehicle almost before it rolled to a stop. He rushed by the surprised valet, leaving the man staring questioningly after him.

With long, hurried strides he took the steps two at a time and entered the double glass doors of the building. Stalking to the lobby desk, he glowered at the young woman who stood there.

"I need a key to Miss Kelton's apartment," he demanded in a breath, holding out his hand.

"I'm sorry, sir, but that's impossible." The pretty blonde turned to place a stack of mail on the desk behind her. "Miss Kelton has given this establishment no such instructions, and without—"

"Dammit, woman, the key!" Jason stormed, slamming his fist on the counter.

His actions caused the woman to jump noticeably, and she stepped back quickly, her face paling, her eyes wide with fright.

"Look, who—whoever you are—"

"The name is Jason Banning!" he gritted. "I own this building, and I demand the key to 403!"

"Right." The woman smiled weakly and looked around for help, certain she had a nut case to contend with. Trying to pacify him, she started trying to soothe him "Well, ah, Mr. Banning, is it? If you'll just— Hey!" she shouted when

Jason ignored her, rounded the counter and pulled open the bottom drawer of the desk and rummaged through it. "You can't do that!"

"Can't I?" Jason differed, his green eyes glittering as they challenged her. He withdrew his hand and in it triumphantly held the passkey. Slamming the drawer shut, he headed for the elevator. He glanced back over his shoulder in grim amusement to see the woman hurry to the telephone and frantically begin to dial.

The door slid open, and Jason entered the elevator as a stocky gray-haired woman stepped out, smiling broadly.

"Hello, Mr. Banning. How are you this fine day?" she greeted.

"I'm fine, Marie, but the same can't be said for your assistant," Jason returned with a nod of his head toward the white-faced woman sputtering hysterically into the telephone. "Seems to think I'm some kind of loony, and I think she's calling security."

"What!" Marie was aghast. "Oh, Mr. Bann—" Her shocked voice was cut off when the elevator door slid smoothly shut.

Jason left the car at the fourth floor and fairly ran the length of the hall to Corey's apartment.

"Corey!" His voice rang down the corridor ahead of him, and when he reached her door, his fist banged on the barrier. "Corey!" he shouted again.

Quickly Jason inserted the passkey, opened the door and entered the apartment. He glanced around the orderly living room, stuck his head over the swinging café doors of the kitchenette, then headed toward Corey's bedroom.

Stopping short in the doorway, he braced himself, his outstretched hands on the doorframe. His heart stilled in his breast, and he ceased to breathe as his frightened eyes took in the scene before him.

Corey lay in a crumpled heap upon the floor, the telephone receiver dangling only inches from her fingers, the bedclothes trailing from the bed to the floor.

Jason's shocked gaze moved to the bedside table.

"Oh, God, no!" The words tore from his lips when he saw the open medicine bottle lying on its side, pills spilling from the container. Not even realizing he had crossed the room in giant strides, Jason knelt beside Corey and laid his head gently upon her breast to listen for the reassuring heartbeat. At the same time, his fingertips were upon her inner wrist, feeling for the pulse that beat steadily under his touch.

With a long, ragged sigh of tremendous relief, he lifted her into his embrace and slowly rose with Corey's limp body in his arms and sank to the bed.

"Corey, can you hear me?" he asked, shaking her, willing her to hear him, to respond. "Oh, baby, please wake up!" he pleaded, his voice tormented.

She stirred slightly in his arms.

"Jason?" she breathed, forcing open her heavy eyelids and trying to focus on his face. But her eyes fluttered closed.

"Why, Corey?" he cried, tears misting his eyes. "Why do something so drastic, so senseless? Life's too precious to waste," Jason murmured strickenly, one hand gently stroking the bright hair from her brow. "I won't let you do this, Corey. Do you hear me? I won't!"

"So tired," she whispered faintly, "couldn't sleep...took something...to help me sleep."

"How many, Corey?" he yelled hoarsely. "The pills! How many did you take?" When she didn't respond, he shook her again. *"How many sleeping pills did you take, dammit!"*

"W-what?" She struggled to sit up, only to fall back weakly against his shoulder.

"How many pills did you take?" he repeated more patiently, watching her alertly.

"One," Corey replied feebly, "just one, I think...."

"God, I hope you're telling the truth," Jason breathed, releasing his hold on her to reach for the overturned bottle, his eyes scanning the label for the prescription date. Yesterday. He read on to find the quantity. Fifteen. Quickly emptying the remaining pills onto the table, he began to count them...twelve...thirteen...fourteen.

"Thank God!" Jason breathed as he dropped the last pellet into the bottle and snapped the plastic lid shut. He laughed openly as a single tear coursed its way down his cheek. "You scared the hell out of me! I thought I'd lost you—lost you before I ever had the chance to have you."

He settled himself upon the bed, gathered Corey's unresisting body into his arms and crushed her to him, rocking her as if she were a baby. Then he placed a kiss upon her brow and whispered, "Sleep, little one. Sleep."

Jason sat holding Corey for an endless time, afraid to move, to let her go. God! What horror had gone through his mind, his heart, when he had seen her seemingly lifeless form on the floor! He had gone through hell in the brief time it had taken him just to cross the room and find that she was breathing.

He looked down at the sleeping woman who lay so trustingly in his arms, noting that some of the tiredness had been erased from her lovely face. She seemed so relaxed, and he wondered with wry amusement what she would do if she realized that she was nestled contentedly against his breast.

Jason's lips curled in a half smile, recalling Corey's unreasonable aversion to him. Their love scenes had given him an opportunity to touch Corey, to hold her close to his heart, to kiss her divinely sweet lips, despite her declared feelings.

He could really have let himself go and thoroughly enjoyed the scenes, had Corey cooperated. Instead he had felt her cold animosity; at other times, her feverish rebellion. And always, her thinly veiled bitterness and hatred.

Lurking within the depths of her tawny eyes was the constant accusation that Jason was directly responsible for Matt Fielder's death and the subsequent takeover of the studios, which Corey believed to belong to her and Cappy, jointly.

How could he convince her of the truth? What would it take for her to accept the fact that he, Jason Banning, would never do anything to hurt her? Would she ever see the love for her in his clear eyes, ever know how he welcomed the love scenes and the chance to declare his passionate love? That he was *not* merely acting but taking full advantage of each one to try and break down the barrier of hostility she had erected between them?

With a heavy sigh he recalled their parting the night before, the words that had been flung between them. He remembered Cappy questioning him this morning... *Cappy!*

Jason had promised to let him know immediately if he found Corey. He would be distraught by this time, while Jason sat at ease upon Corey's bed, propped against the headboard, with soft pillows at his back and the sleeping beauty in his arms.

He managed to shift Corey from his lap to the bed without rousing her from her deep slumber. He heard her moan softly and watched as she turned on her side, drawing her knees upward to curl into a fetal position, one loose fist lying against her satiny cheek.

Jason eased himself from the bed and stood looking down at Corey, his gaze leisurely traveling over the woman on the bed. The ice-blue silk wrap she wore clung to the soft curves of her body and teased his senses, hinting at the wonders it concealed, and something seemed to uncoil from deep within him to spiral through his entire being. He had the urge to lie close beside her, fitting her body to his own, and hold her until she awakened.

He shook his dark head as if to clear it and, feeling guilty that he had not already done so, reached down to retrieve the fallen telephone receiver and dialed Cappy at the studio office. He heard only one short ring before the breathless voice of the director answered.

"Cappy here!"

"Jason Banning, Cappy," he began in a hushed tone. "Sorry to be so long in reporting, but Corey is fine."

"You're sure she's all right, Jason?" came the worried question.

"She's fine, Cappy," Jason assured the older man.

"Will you be coming back here soon?"

"No. I'll be hanging around here for a while," Jason returned, then added, "Don't expect Corey, either. She won't be coming in today, Cappy. I suggest that you go ahead with the shoot, working around Corey and me."

"You aren't telling me everything, Jason. If Corey's—"

"She's getting some much-needed and long overdue rest, my friend, that's all. There's nothing to worry about."

There was a long pause before Cappy's heavy sigh broke the silence.

"Thanks for calling, Jason, and letting me know she's all right."

Jason stood for a moment holding the receiver, a thoughtful expression on his handsome face. Then he leaned forward to pull the telephone cord from the wall jack and replaced the receiver on the now-dead instrument.

He sat heavily on the chair near Corey's bed and removed his shoes. With a weary sigh he closed his eyes and leaned his head on the headrest. He, too, was tired, having put in as many hours as Corey on the set, then working in his office at the studio after everyone else had gone. Most nights he had not gone home, catching a few winks on the couch in the office.

After a few minutes of trying, and failing, to make himself comfortable and relax, Jason opened his eyes and looked longingly at the bed.

On a sudden impulse he obeyed the urge he had had earlier and rose quickly to move to the bed. He eased himself down and stretched his length beside the sleeping woman, then molded his body to fit the curve of hers, her back resting gently against him. Carefully he placed an arm across Corey and felt her snuggle closer to him, completely unaware of her action.

How often had he dreamed of holding her like this? How many times had he wished her to be pliable in his arms during their love scenes? How many times he had willed her to be receptive to his touch, his kisses?

Corey stirred, and Jason immediately released his hold, removing his arm from around her. Unaware of the tenseness of his body, he slowly expelled the breath he hadn't known he was holding and watched the still-sleeping woman.

She rolled from her side onto her back, and the ice-blue silk wrap stretched tightly across her firm breasts, drawing his attention. He caught his breath sharply when she nestled closer against his warmth. A slight, almost purring sound came from her throat as once again she settled into the depths of slumber.

His body responded, desire stirring within. God! He wouldn't be able to lie here with Corey and not touch her. Taking a deep breath, he eased away from her and stood looking down at her. He reached out to pull the covers over her, then leaned down to brush her brow with a feathery kiss and left the room.

* * *

The warm rays of late-afternoon sun filtered through the powder-blue eyelet drapes of the bedroom window as Corey slowly returned to wakefulness. Her eyelids seemed to be weighted, her body heavy, and for a moment she felt strangely giddy. Rubbing a hand across her face, she grimaced as she noted the aftertaste of the sleeping pill.

Turning her head took quite an effort, but she managed a glimpse at the bedside clock and realized that she had missed her morning call to work. Also, her bedroom was on the west side of the building, and the sun never streamed into her bedroom window in the mornings!

With a start Corey realized that she had slept most of the day and made haste to rise from her bed. A sound caught her attention, and she stood still, listening. Again she heard it and knew that it came from the direction of her kitchen.

Someone was in her house. A burglar! Corey glanced about the room, her gaze resting on a large crystal vase on her bureau. Moving noiselessly, she reached for it, then her fingers tightened about the cool glass. Then she cautiously made her way toward the sound of the intruder.

Once again the sound came, and she stopped, her head crooked to one side as she listened. She recognized the rattle of pots and pans. What would a burglar want with her cooking pots? The rich aroma of fresh coffee assailed her nostrils: the burglar was making coffee!

Corey tiptoed toward the kitchen and paused just at the doorway to lean forward, her gaze scanning the small room. Knowing that her cooking utensils were in the cabinet under the breakfast bar, she realized that the person had to be there. Her bare feet soundless on the wooden floor, she crept around the bar, her weapon poised above her head, ready to strike.

Broad shoulders stretched taut beneath a red-and-black checkered flannel shirt, muscular thighs knotted and strained against tight-fitting faded jeans as the crouching man rummaged in the cabinet, his head lowered out of sight.

Corey took a guarded step forward and stopped short when a dark head emerged. Now was her time. She had to make her move before he did. She took a deep breath, gritted her teeth and, with her eyes tightly closed, brought the heavy vase downward.

"Hey!" a startled voice yelled out.

There was a loud thud, the sound of crystal shattering, then silence. An eerie quiet suspended in time.

Corey released her breath loudly and stood trembling, afraid to open her eyes. Dear God! What if she had killed him? She groaned and suddenly felt sick. Then came the sound of a movement, and her eyes flew open to stare wide-eyed at her victim.

His broad shoulders were at an angle at her, his folded arms covered his face and cradled his dark head in protection. His shirt was covered with fragments of glass and when he stirred, the shards rained down to settle on the floor about him.

"Damn! What in hell—" the man sputtered angrily as he came to his feet, shaking himself free of more broken glass. "What is it with you?" he demanded as he towered over her.

Corey stifled a cry of surprise and stared with horror into the stormy eyes of Jason Banning.

"Damn you, Corey, you could have killed me!" Jason reached out, grasped her shoulders with his strong grip and shook her firmly. "Why would you—"

"I-I thought you were..." she choked in a whisper, her eyes misting. "I woke up and heard noises. I thought it was a burglar."

Jason saw the tears shimmering in her eyes, her small teeth biting her lower lip, the trembling of her chin, and eased his hold. Of course! When she had woken, she had

had no way of knowing who was there. She'd simply been attempting to protect herself.

"I'm sorry, Jason," Corey breathed, her gaze locked with his. "You're right. I might have hurt you badly."

"It's all right, Corey," he assured her gently. "You were only trying to protect yourself. You couldn't have known it was me."

The hushed softness of Jason's voice flowed over her like warm honey, causing her heart to quicken its beat. His hands slipped from her shoulders to glide downward over her arms to her trembling hands. With a gentle squeeze of her hands, he released them to caress her slender waist.

Corey started at his touch, for it seemed to burn through the cool silk of her wrap. She stared at his sensuous mouth and the faint half smile touching his lips and a tremor raced hotly through her veins. She held her breath as his dark gaze slowly traced her face, then moved on to make a lengthy inspection of her body. She sensed the passion that forever lurked just beneath the surface—a passion that would take little to ignite. She felt the stirrings of her own desire, and on its heels came fright. She tried to pull free of his hold.

"No, don't move," Jason warned, tightening his arms about her.

"Let go of me!" she cried with alarm, mistaking his intention, afraid more of herself and of her awakening arousal than fearful of Jason. In her panic she fought against him. "Jason, let me go!"

"Hold still, Corey!" Jason cautioned lifting her off the floor despite her renewed struggle. "Dammit, you idiot, I'm not going to attack you!" He felt her body instantly stiffen, and her shocked eyes met his. "You were about to cut yourself," he informed her calmly, seating her none too gently on one of the high-backed bar stools. "You're barefoot," he continued, pointing to her feet, "and there's glass all over the floor."

"Oh" was all she managed, embarrassed that she had misread his reluctance to release her, humiliated by her senseless fear and stupid reaction to the situation.

"Speaking of glass, my shirt is covered with slivers," he went on. "Your aim isn't too good. You hit the counter with a solid blow. With all that power behind it, I'm just glad you missed my head," Jason ended with a laugh, pulling his shirttail from his jeans, then beginning to unbutton his shirt.

Corey was unable to restrain her wayward gaze. Like a magnet it was drawn to the simple yet somehow sensual movement of Jason's strong tanned fingers as they worked the buttons of his shirt. She didn't so much as blink so enthralled was she.

Beautiful! She caught her breath at the sight of his bare chest. Lord, but he was beautiful. There was no other word, no other way to describe the perfection of the man. Powerless to do anything other than stare openly, she drank in the magnificence of his broad, powerful chest and flat belly, taut with muscles.

Jason's skin was a deep bronze, and the fluid play of perfectly toned muscles rippled as he moved. Spellbound and breathless, Corey felt desire coiling within her. She closed her hands tightly into fists, stilling the impulse to reach out, to touch the beauty that had captivated her. She yearned to stroke the mat of black hair that accented his chest and tapered to his belly to trail downward beyond his waistband.

There *was* such a thing as "male beauty," for Jason Banning was living proof!

Noting Corey's rapt attention to his physique and correctly reading the hunger in her tawny eyes, Jason sucked in his breath, desire awakening in his loins and mounting fast. His heart pounded like a sledgehammer in his chest.

Although she held her body stiff and unmoving, he had watched her bright eyes follow his every movement, had heard her draw in her breath sharply and was acutely aware of the pulse in her smooth neck throbbing noticeably. But when he saw her moisten her lips with the tip of her pink tongue, that was just about his undoing!

Jason reined in his emotions as best he could, which was no easy task with Corey looking at him as if she might suddenly pounce on and devour him! The raw hunger in her eyes! There was a fire roaring within him, licking hotly through his veins with a danger of burning out of control. His fingers itched to touch her, to feel the heat of her passion. And it was there, all right, in every word she didn't speak, in every move she didn't make.

Her firm, rounded breasts moved with every quick breath, their dusky nipples hardened with desire and pressed against the silken wrap, beckoning his touch. He felt the urgency in his own body building to fever pitch, his manhood stirring to life, protesting against the confining jeans.

"Damn!" Jason's sudden curse caused them both to jump, and he turned from Corey, willing self-control. "Where do you keep the broom and dustpan?" he asked tightly.

"The pantry, there to your right," she answered a little too loudly, her own emotions surging through her. "But I can clean up this mess, Jason. After all, I made it, and if you'd—"

"I'll do it!" he declared, his body rigid. As he glanced over his shoulder at her, their gazes met and held. "You'd best get some clothes on," he advised in a strange, almost strangled voice. "And some shoes," he added as he opened the pantry door.

Corey eased herself off the stool but made no move to leave. She ran her fingers shakily through her unruly mane of chestnut hair and watched as Jason bent and began to pick up the largest pieces of the broken glass and put them in the dustpan. Once he glanced up at her, pinning her with his emerald stare, then without a word went back to his task.

Corey breathed a deep sigh, turned and headed for her bedroom. Upon closing the door, she leaned her head against it, her knees weak, her mind confused. The rapid beating of her heart refused to resume its normal pace.

On trembling legs she crossed to the bed and sat down, shaking her head as if to clear it. She had to think, get her emotions in check, and she certainly had to cool the heat that raged through her like wildfire.

So many questions crowded her mind. . . .

Why did Jason Banning have this staggering effect on her? With all her bitterness, her hostility, her utter dislike of him, why did desire flame within her any time she came within ten feet of him? Dammit, why did her body forever respond to him, forever betray her?

And what was Jason doing in her house, anyway? How had he gotten in? Why hadn't she asked him?

Corey sprang from the bed and stalked to the door, pausing with her hand on the doorknob. Unbidden came the picture of Jason sprawled on her kitchen floor, bleeding, unconscious, even dead— She paled suddenly. Lord, she might have killed him! The thought made her stomach lurch and caused her throat to tighten painfully. She made her way back to the bed unsteadily.

Why hadn't she demanded the answers when she'd realized it was Jason and not some stranger in her kitchen? Why hadn't she been angry when she had found him in her house? Had she accepted his being there without question because she unknowingly wanted him there? No matter how she fought her attraction to Jason, in truth *did* she want him?

"Why *are* you here, Jason?" she whispered to the empty room.

Corey looked at the digital clock and saw that it read 5:40 p.m. It would soon be evening. He must have came over to see why she hadn't shown up for work, she reasoned. But he could have called.

Glancing at the telephone, Corey saw that it was unplugged. And *she* hadn't unplugged it! Of that she was certain. So it had to have been Jason. But why? Why had he let her sleep? Why hadn't he preached fire and brimstone about her oversleeping, missing work and costing Banning Productions time and money?

Corey's questioning thoughts slid to a halt when from the living room she heard the balcony door sliding open. There followed the muffled sound of cloth being snapped in the wind a few times, then one last time. Jason was shaking the glass out of his shirt. Then she heard the door slide closed, the snap of the lock, and she smiled when Jason's carefree whistle drifted through her apartment. He didn't seem to be very upset at the fact that she'd just done her best to brain him.

Corey went into the bathroom, shed her silk wrap and stepped into the shower. The cold blast stung her heated skin, and she stood there for long moments, the spray needling her face and body. What was it about the stridently sexy man that made her respond to him? Why did Jason have a sexual allure, an appeal that so captivated her it drew her to him without reason?

Dressed in jeans and an oversize rust-colored sweater, Corey padded on stocking feet toward the kitchen, with a pair of soft leather moccasins in hand. She entered the kitchen, dropped the shoes to the floor, slipped her feet into them and sat down at the breakfast bar.

Immediately Jason set a mug of coffee on the counter before her, and Corey spooned in two teaspoons of sugar, sipped the rich, hot liquid and sighed.

"Good?" he asked, crooking a dark eyebrow inquiringly.

"Very good," she answered honestly. Cupping the mug in both hands, she blew into its heated contents and inhaled the scent. Over the rim of her mug, she studied the man only a few feet away, observing him quietly as Jason strode to the refrigerator and removed a carton of eggs and a jug of milk, going about the business of cooking.

She had never watched a man cook before and was amazed at how comfortable he seemed to be. His movements were totally natural, and he seemed completely at ease. The few men she had dated had been at a loss in the kitchen, cringing at the mere suggestion that they help to clear the table and wash the dishes. And cook? Never! It wasn't masculine. But Jason was extremely masculine, even in the kitchen.

A faint smile tugged at Corey's lips. Even in the feminine white apron with little red hearts sprinkled over it, Jason Banning was sexy! He was shirtless, and she watched with fascination the play of muscles and tanned flesh. She chuckled softly at the sight.

The sound of Corey's breathy laugh alerted Jason, and he turned to see her watching him, a bright smile on her lovely face. His green eyes moved lazily over her, and a slight smile played over his own lips.

"Does the lady find something amusing?" he inquired, raising a dark eyebrow indignantly.

"I would never have thought it possible," she announced, with laughter in her voice.

"What?" he asked, turning back to the stove.

"Cooking, being in a kitchen, acting as if he were born to it. In short, it's hard to imagine you as being domestic."

"Well, to tell you the truth, I've always enjoyed the art of cooking," he told her with a deep chuckle. The sound was warm with contentment. "I shocked a lot of my friends when I took a course in cooking. At the time it was purely for survival, but I enjoyed it so much that I went a step further." He turned to Corey, a disarming smile on his full lips, and bowed exaggeratedly. Then, straightening to his full height, he patted himself on his aproned chest and announced, "I, Jason Banning, am a bona fide gourmet cook."

"No!" Corey feigned shock, her tawny eyes wide. "For real?"

"Yes, Miss Kelton, for real. Many would say it was unmanly—"

"I think it's sexy," she whispered and made herself busy with the plates and silverware on the bar.

"I'm sorry? I didn't hear you. You think it's what?" Jason pressed with an engaging grin.

Corey hesitantly repeated in a low voice, "I said I think it's sexy."

"What?" Jason queried with interest. "Did you say you think I'm sexy?"

"Not you, that is, not just you. I think it's sexy...you know, a man in the kitchen, knowing how to take charge and be at ease."

"So you like a man who takes charge, huh?" Jason asked teasingly. He grinned wickedly at her, then laughed heartily at her flush of embarrassment.

Corey made no attempt to answer his question, merely shot him a quick look and bristled at his laughter. She watched with interest as he chopped onions, red chili peppers, mushrooms, tomatoes and avocado into a bowl, then put it beside a cup of grated cheese.

Jason one-handedly broke eggs into a mixing bowl, added a bit of milk and beat the mixture into a pale yellow froth before pouring it into a generously buttered pan heating on the stove. He tossed the chopped vegetables into the egg mixture, followed with the cheese and topped it off with a sprinkling of crisp bacon bits.

A delicious aroma wafted about the kitchen and made Corey's mouth water and her stomach growl with hunger. Within minutes Jason slid a lightly browned omelet from the pan onto her waiting plate. He repeated the procedure as before, and while his own omelet cooked, he removed warmed flour tortillas and a platter of golden-brown home-fries from the oven. Returning to the refrigerator, he retrieved a bottle of hot sauce and a pitcher of freshly squeezed orange juice.

His omelet now ready, he slipped it onto his plate, rounded the bar and seated himself beside Corey. Before he began to eat, he picked up the pitcher of juice and filled the two juice glasses resting on the bar.

"More coffee?" Jason asked then, reaching for the coffeepot, his voice cheerful, his dark eyes dancing with good humor.

"Please." And when he had refilled her mug, Corey murmured a husky "Thank you."

"My pleasure, ma'am," Jason drawled, inclining his head. "You like my coffee; now lets see if it's likewise with my cooking."

Corey cut into her omelet, put a bite into her mouth and slowly savored the delectable taste. It was wonderful, light, seasoned just right, and nearly melted in her mouth. She cut into it once again, opened her mouth and stopped, her fork poised in midair. She glanced sideways to see Jason watching her with interest, an inquiring look on his handsome face.

"Well?" he queried.

"Well, what?" she returned, still holding her fork in the air.

"What do you think?"

"It's fine."

"Fine?" Reaching out his hand, he closed it over hers and brought the fork to his own mouth, taking her bite of omelet. "Just 'fine'?"

"Yes, fine," she returned, laughter again touching her voice. She smiled at his look of exasperation, knowing full well Jason wanted to hear his culinary efforts highly complimented. Deliberately she withheld any word of praise.

"Thank you—I think." He released her hand and turned to his own plate. He cut into his omelet savagely, mumbling under his breath.

"Well, what do you want, Jason?" Corey questioned, amused at his display. He reminded her of a little boy who had completed a project and had received only a little praise, when he had expected more.

When he didn't answer, she chided, "Now, that's not sexy!"

"What's not?" he questioned in a puzzled tone, staring at Corey with wide green eyes. When there was no reply, he demanded, "What isn't sexy?" Again she didn't answer. "Are you telling me my food isn't sexy?"

"No, your pouting—it isn't sexy. Your food—"

"'Pouting'? Pouting!" he snapped, still staring at her. He saw her arch a fine eyebrow at his discomfiture. "I'm not pouting, dammit!" he growled.

"No?"

"No!"

They ate on in silence. Only the tinkling sounds of glass and silverware cut the quiet. Once Corey glanced at Jason to find his green eyes fixed on her, but they slid quickly away. She reached for the juice pitcher at the same time he did, and their hands touched the handle at the same time. Simultaneously there came incoherent mumbles of apology as they removed their hands as if they had touched something hot.

At length Corey pushed her empty plate away, downed the last of her coffee and sighed with contentment.

"On a scale of one to ten," she began slowly, then left the sentence hanging as she poured more coffee and added sugar. Bringing the mug to her lips, she sipped the liquid, meeting Jason's open stare. "I'd have to rate the coffee a perfect ten." She smiled and continued. "Service? Another ten, and the food..."

"Was fine," Jason mumbled, pushing his own plate back.

"And the food," she went on, as if he had not spoken, "I'd rate no less than a ten and a half, maybe even an eleven."

Jason's face brightened as a smile lit his eyes and spread to his sensuous lips. The hint of a dimple played at the left corner of his mouth, and Corey's heart skipped a beat.

"That good, huh?" he queried easily, obviously pleased with her words.

"That good," she repeated simply.

When he merely sat there with that heart-stopping smile on his handsome face, Corey nervously stood and began busying herself with clearing the breakfast bar. When she reached for the soiled plates, her hands shook noticeably, and she knocked over her coffee mug, making a small puddle on the butcher-block counter. Wordlessly she watched as Jason leaned forward and dabbed at the spill with his napkin, wiping the countertop before placing the soiled napkin on top of the plates she held in her hands.

"How did you get into my apartment?" Corey asked suddenly.

"With a key," Jason answered matter-of-factly, leaning back comfortably in his chair.

"A key?" Placing the dishes in the sink with a clatter, she turned wide, questioning eyes on him. "B-but how? Cappy? Did he give you his key?" she stammered.

"Cappy has a key to your place?" Jason sat forward with a start, his eyes narrowing, his body taut.

"Of course he does," Corey stated without hesitation. Then, reading his obvious thoughts, her face washed with color. "It isn't what you're thinking, Jason Banning!" she snapped heatedly, her hands on her hips. "Cappy is my best friend! He is a father, a brother, a friend, all rolled into one heck of a nice guy!"

"If you say so," Jason muttered, raising one dark eyebrow in disbelief.

"Well, I do!" she shot back, her temper rising. "And my relationship with him is none of your business, in the first place. And in the second place," she said, her voice rising by degrees, "I don't know why I'm explaining *anything* to you. If anyone should be explaining, it's you! So, Mr. Banning, just how in the hell *did* you obtain a key to my house?" she demanded.

"I borrowed a passkey from management."

"Of course you did," Corey agreed sarcastically and gave a small, mirthless laugh as she whisked a wayward tress of hair from her face. "Why didn't I realize that? You simply waltzed into a highly secure building—"

"Stormed in," he corrected easily.

"Requested a key to my apartment—"

"Demanded one."

"Was given said key—"

"I took it."

"And no one called security—"

"Someone was in the act of calling the guards when I left the lobby."

"You got on the elevator—"

"That part you got right."

"And no one tried to stop you?"

"No one."

"Right!" Corey concurred icily. "And I'm the Queen of Sheba!"

"You are? No kidding?" he responded, his green eyes wide with pretended amazement, then chuckled throatily.

"Jason Banning, how did you get a key to my apartment?" she bit out heatedly, stamping her small foot in angry frustration, her fists clenched at her sides.

"From management," Jason repeated calmly. With a sigh, he added, "No one stopped me, Corey, because I own this building."

Stupefied, Corey merely stared at Jason as she absorbed the impact of his words. She stood as if in shock, stunned into motionlessness. She was speechless, unable to command her body to react. As hard as she tried, she had neither the ability nor the power to move or speak.

"Corey?" His voice a husky, intimate whisper, Jason tenderly brushed a wayward tendril from her brow and trailed a forefinger along her cheek. "Why are you asking how I got in now? Why didn't you ask when you first saw me?" he questioned softly.

Hadn't she asked herself the same thing? How could she respond to Jason when she hadn't been able to answer that question herself? Why, indeed?

"Corey?"

Slowly Corey raised her eyes to his, battling with her confusion, her emotions. "I-I don't know," she replied truthfully. "I've asked myself, and I haven't been able to find the answer."

Jason drew her into his embrace, his lips hovering near Corey's, his breath warm upon her face. "The answer is there, honey," he whispered against her lips. "You'll find it if you try."

"Jason—" She drew in her breath sharply when he stilled her words by running his tongue along her bottom lip. A deep, familiar pain tugged at her heart, desire stirred, and a moan rose in her throat. She made to push away from him, but Jason tightened his hold, bringing her closer to him.

"Feel it, Corey? The ache, the hunger, the need? That's desire, the promise of passion," he breathed. "My God, don't tell me you don't feel the passion that's between us!"

"I can't," she denied, struggling to get free. "I-I won't! Oh, Jason, please don't do this to me," she pleaded, desire overwhelming her, threatening to win over reason.

"What about what you're doing to me, Corey?" Jason demanded. Setting her from him, his hands gripped her upper arms, and he pinned her with the heat and intensity of his green eyes. "Desire is a fact of life; it's reality. I want you, Corey. That is fact—reality. Another fact, and equally important, is that you want me!"

"No I don't."

"Yes, you do!" he countered. "Look at you. You're on fire you ache—"

"No!" Corey screamed, pulling free and moving away from him on trembling legs, her heart pounding painfully in her breast.

"Corey, listen to me," Jason said urgently, taking a step nearer her.

"Don't," she snapped, her hands raised and outstretched as if to ward him off. "Leave me alone—don't touch me."

"Don't touch you?" he asked gently, not coming any nearer. "What are you afraid of, Corey? Me? Yourself? Or is it that you are terrified of what we are together?"

"I'm afraid of nothing."

"Oh, but you are," he countered with a wistful sigh.

Jason turned suddenly and strode from the kitchen, then through the living room and stopped only to retrieve his lightweight jacket from the coatrack. Standing in the doorway, he glanced over his shoulder at Corey. "I'm honest enough to admit I want you. And I've seen desire in a woman's eyes too many times not to be able to recognize it. Don't fight the inevitable, Corey; you're merely feeding the fire. And the fire is there, between us. We both know it; we've both felt it. We'll be touched by that fire again, and don't you doubt it for one minute!''

And with that he walked out, leaving a shaken Corey staring in consternation at the closed door.

Seven

With a practiced eye Corey scanned the pages of the revised manuscript, pondering for the millionth time why the writer had changed the script again. She'd seen nothing wrong with the original story: in fact she'd thought it to be very good. But more than once she had heard comments about how "moody," "temperamental" and "given to change" writers were.

Corey sighed wearily and massaged the tightening muscles in the back of her neck. She would simply have to resign herself to the changes and face the fact that she would have to study the script and relearn her lines.

From her secluded spot in the rear of the studio she heard the rhythmic hum of voices of the cast and crew as they shot a scene in which she did not appear. She was blessed with time to herself and had found a place beyond the whirl of shooting and action. She sat on the wooden floor amid a tangle of cables, discarded props and general junk.

Tossing the bulky script aside, she leaned back against a small mountain of heavy ropes and stretched her legs out to prop her feet on a speaker box. Comfortable with her resting place, she closed her eyes in an attempt to relax, to block out everything and everyone about her.

Suddenly Corey was keenly aware of one voice among the drone of the others. The deep, throaty sound caused her heart to race, and a familiar heat flowed through her body, followed by a tingling sensation. She was conscious of a tightening in her chest.

Jason.

It was always the same. The effect he had on her was uncanny. Immediately mental pictures of Jason Banning flashed on the screen of her mind: the same pictures that had been plaguing her waking thoughts and had followed her into her dreams. Jason, standing in her kitchen, wearing her apron, cooking. Jason, fishing for a compliment on his culinary prowess, the little-boy pout. Jason, pinning her with the intense heat of his emerald stare and bluntly declaring that he wanted her.

She felt again the frustration, the fear, and yes, the *desire* she had experienced when he had stated in that husky, velvety voice that she wanted him. The tension had mounted, had hung so thickly that one could almost have reached out and touched it. Then he had left, walked out the door without another word. But not without a parting dart from eyes shooting green fire that met its target, piercing her heart with its flame to burn hot and deep within.

In the week that had followed, there had been no mention, not one single indication, not even the slightest hint from either of them that the incident had occurred. But they were equally acutely aware that it had. In every word that wasn't spoken, in every glance and every touch, the remembrance was brought forcibly to each of them. And it was maddening.

"Jason acts as if nothing had happened between us," she muttered. "Ah, come on, Corey," she reminded herself gruffly, "nothing *did* happen."

But, she thought, that didn't mean that something couldn't have—wouldn't have! Was that it? Was that what was so upsetting? she questioned in aggravation. Had she wanted something to happen and because nothing had... *Ooh*, it was all too confusing. But what if—

"What if! If! Dammit, Corey, your whole life has been 'what ifs'!" she murmured brokenly. "When will you learn? When will you—"

"Rehearsing your lines, beautiful? Or have you taken to talking to yourself?"

The unexpected sound of Jason's baritone voice startled Corey, and she sat bolt upright. In her abrupt movement she knocked over the speaker with a loud crash that echoed across the large studio. Heads turned, and silence settled over the room.

Somehow Corey managed to become entangled in the ropes and fought at the offending cordage, a whimpering sound clawing its way upward through her throat and escaping her lips.

"Corey, hold still," Jason cautioned gently, his hands on her shoulders.

The warmth of his touch spiraled through her, and her breath caught sharply, painfully. Their gazes locked. Jason stiffened noticeably. Corey trembled uncontrollably.

"D-don't touch me. Please don't touch me," she pleaded brokenly.

The plea had been meant to be a silent one, but when he had touched her, a flame had leaped, a fire sparked within her, and in her confusion she had unintentionally spoken the words aloud.

"You've got it, lady," he said coldly. He stood looking down at her, and a cool mask of aloofness claimed his handsome face. When he spoke again, both his words and his tone were blunt and chilling. "If you've had sufficient time to study your lines, Miss Kelton, you're needed on the set. That is, if you can find the time and can pull yourself away from indulging in daydreams. After all, we do have a deadline to meet."

Corey watched as Jason stalked away, his body rigid with leashed anger. But there had been something else. It had been there in his eyes before they had clouded with icy indifference. It had been only a flicker, but it had been there, nevertheless.

What was it? Corey wondered in frustration as she extracted herself from the snarl of ropes. She reached for the script and scrambled to her feet but made no move to follow Jason, so lost was she in her musing.

"When Miss Kelton decides to join us..." Jason intoned acidly.

The sound of his voice snapped Corey back to the situation at hand. Once again the completion of the film seemed to be uppermost in his mind, the most important thing in his world.

She stormed across the studio. Slamming the script on a nearby table, she marched to the place Cappy indicated. Her hands on her shapely hips, she tapped the floor with her foot in a frenzy of impatience as Jason spoke his lines.

"I'll have no more, wife," he bellowed, in his own anger. "This bickering, this—this show of spirit. Enough!"

Taking a deep, steadying breath, Corey delivered her lines with relish. Her fiery anger flared as she glared at Jason, her tawny eyes spitting golden fire.

"You'll have no more. You!" she spat, moving to stand mere inches away from him.

"Curb your tongue, woman," came the low warning. "I am the master here!"

"Master?" Corey countered, her face flushed. *"I have no master."* Tilting her head back, she fastened him with a surly stare and jabbed her forefinger hard and repeatedly at his broad chest, an action that was not in the script. "You are arrogant, pompous, insolent and downright insufferable."

In her very real anger toward the man who stood before her, rather than the anger she was supposed to have toward the character he portrayed, she became caught up in her rampage.

"You are..." Corey faltered when she felt herself drowning, lost in Jason's emerald stare. She was held spellbound, oblivious to everything and everyone about them. For the moment, they were the only two in the room. She swallowed with difficulty, blinked once, twice, shook her head as if to clear it.

Where was she? she wondered, trying desperately to remember her lines. Oh, yes, now she remembered and resumed speaking.

"You are the most..."

There was the most exciting, enticing, purely sexual light burning in Jason's eyes. Corey's gaze scanned his handsome face, noting the slight flaring of his nostrils, the lazy, almost dreamy smile on his full lips, the lock of hair that refused to be tamed and fell over his brow.

Although her hand had ceased its assault on his chest, it remained there, and she could feel the steady rhythm of his heartbeat beneath her fingertips. The musky male scent of him reached out to her, making her dizzy and short of breath.

Once more she found her voice. "You are the most obstinate, unyielding, overbearing man I have ever had the misfortune to meet!" she managed, moving closer to him. "Jason?" she breathed his name, her breath fanning his lips as she spoke, and as if in a trance, Corey reached up, burying her fingers in the thickness of his hair and pulled him closer. "Jason, I—" The husky words were cut off as their lips met.

Beneath his, her own lips trembled as she parted them, her moist tongue shy at first as it traced his lower lip. She gently nipped at the tender flesh coaxingly. A tiny whimper rattled in her throat, and Jason was lost.

"Ah, God, Corey!" The words tore from him in a heated rush, and with a groan that seemed to escape from the depths of his soul, he shuddered as he crushed Corey to the length of his rock-hard body, and his mouth closed over hers in a hungry kiss.

Jason couldn't believe what was happening. He was dreaming, for only in his dreams had Corey reached out to him, kissed him with unrestrained passion. Dream or reality, he wished the kiss would go on forever!

It was an urgent, demanding kiss, and Jason's heart pounded like a wild thing in his breast. Corey melted against him, clung to him, returning the kiss with a fervor that caused a painfully sweet fire to coil in his belly. Its heat rushed forth, searing through his veins.

Corey moved in a sensual, maddening rhythm against him, her soft form melting along the hard contours of his body. His hands slid over her back and along her sides, coming to rest on the firm curve of her buttocks. He pressed her to him intimately, and the fire began to roar within him. And with it came danger. She was driving him crazy! Driving him steadfastly toward the point of no return.

Reality was only a memory, a shadowy, hazy place in the distance. He found himself deep in the pool of the quicksand of passion, and he was sinking rapidly. Slowly he remembered where they were as the fog of desire began to clear. *For God's sake, Banning, you're standing smack-dab in the middle of a roomful of people, and you can damned well bet they're getting an eyeful! Control, Banning,* he warned himself. *Control!*

Reluctantly he pulled himself from the depths of passion and broke the kiss. Lifting his head slowly, he stared down at Corey's flushed face. His heart slammed against his chest when he met her passion-clouded eyes. Her kiss-bruised lips smiled dreamily.

"Once again, Corey, you've deviated from the script," Jason said quietly, his voice noticeably shaky.

Corey stood staring at him, speechless. What had ever possessed her to do such a thing? For the first time she had invited an intimacy between them. There had been no rationale in her action. There had been no stopping the sensual yearning: all she could remember was Jason's emerald eyes and the hypnotic fire that burned within them, setting her body ablaze.

Corey stepped from the shower and vigorously rubbed her wet body with a bath towel, her thoughts tumbling, her mind replaying the intimate kiss she had shared with Jason.

Tossing the towel into a wicker hamper, she snapped off the bathroom light and crossed her bedroom to throw back the blue-gray comforter from her bed. Still naked, she slipped between the cool sheets, hoping they would cool her flushed body.

Would she ever forget that kiss? The way her treacherous body had responded to Jason's touch? Would she ever forget the feel of his strong arms, the hardness of his powerful body? One thing was for certain: she would never forget his response to her nor the passion he generated within her.

For the life of her she couldn't clearly remember what had transpired immediately following the encounter. The rest of the day had passed in a blur. Whatever she had done had been strictly mechanical.

Vaguely she recalled Jason's husky murmur, *"Once again, Corey, you've deviated from the script."* She could almost visualize his green eyes, smoky with confusion and desire.

A delicious shiver ran over Corey's body at the remembrance of Jason's labored breathing, his struggle to maintain control of his passion. It gave her a sense of satisfaction to know that he had been so affected, to know that he had experienced the same sensations she had, that he had waged the same battle of emotions.

Strange, Corey thought, how her thoughts and her feelings toward Jason Banning had changed. It had been a slow, gradual turnaround of her original opinion of the man. Working with him for hours on end, day and night, constantly being thrown together, one on one, Corey had been forced to endure Jason's touch, his embrace, his stage kisses, which had often fanned the smoldering embers of passion into a tiny flame that threatened to ignite a blaze.

And today... Today the scattered pieces of her emotional puzzle had seemed to fall into place. Corey had, in one moment, realized and faced her attraction to Jason Banning, which had been inevitable from the start. In that moment, while she stood drowning in the fathomless pool of his emerald gaze, being drawn to the heat of his being, she was compelled to face the rising passion and the desire that she could no longer deny.

Eight

———

Jason sat slumped behind his desk, wearily eyeing the conglomeration of boxes, files and paperwork that covered his desk and most of the floor. He stacked some papers, snapped a rubber band around them and tossed them into a box that was perched precariously on the edge of a nearby chair.

"Damn! How could *anyone* be this disorganized?" he muttered. "How in heaven's name did he operate under these conditions?"

All morning he had been removing Matt Fielder's belongings, packing them in the boxes and wondering what to do with them. Anything pertaining to the studio—contracts, projects completed or pending, any legal papers—would, of necessity, be retained. The rest he would merely box up and store. It was a distasteful chore that he had deliberately postponed ever since he had taken over Fielder Studios.

He had needed the desk top to work on and at the beginning had simply cleared it, stuffing the items into desk drawers already filled to overflowing in order to have the work space. But the time had come for him to sort through and dispose of Matt's belongings.

Only then, he thought grimly, could he banish Matt from the premises and make the office his own. Often, when one of the cast or crew were attempting to locate an item, he had heard someone say "It's in Matt's office" or "Look in Matt's office." And Corey *always* referred to it that way—whether from habit or intentionally to irritate him, Jason didn't know.

"Well, it's high time for this to become 'Jason's office,'" he said aloud, adding, "As a matter of fact, it's long overdue."

Another thing, his thoughts ran on, the very next thing to do was to have the signs of the grounds and building changed. They should read, Banning Productions, not Fielder Studios. Of course that action would most likely send Corey into a rage, but he'd have to deal with that eventually, so it might just as well be now. After all, business was business.

The thought of Corey's reaction to the change nagged at Jason's mind. She felt that the studios rightfully belonged to Cappy and her, and, although that fact hadn't come up for some time now, Jason knew that it was never far from her mind.

Why did he continually worry about Corey? What did it matter what she thought or felt? Foolish questions, Banning, he admonished himself, knowing full well why it mattered. For caring is a big part of loving. And, fool that he was, he did love Corey Kelton and had for the better part of eight years. He could remember the exact moment it had happened, and he had been unable to do anything about it because she'd only been sixteen!

And what could he do about it now? he wondered anew, running his long, tanned fingers through his mane of dark hair in exasperation. Because of Matt Fielder, this damned studio and the money Corey and Cappy had—

Suddenly Jason reached a long arm across the desk and jabbed the intercom button impatiently.

"Edith!"

"Ye-e-s, handsome?" came the throaty, drawled response.

"Edith, I don't think you'll ever make a proper secretary," Jason returned, laughter in his voice.

"Now, Jason darlin', not once have I ever disappointed you. I know how to please you like *no-o* other—"

"Edith?"

"Yes, Ja-son?"

"Bring your cute little tush in here right now," he ordered.

"Why, Mr. Banning, you're *so* demanding."

Jason cut the connection and leaned back in his leather chair, his green gaze on the door and a devilish smile on his handsome face.

The door opened, and Edith Ward sashayed in and crossed over to stand beside his desk, and when Jason lifted his gaze to meet her cool, green eyes, fringed with red-gold lashes, she winked and puckered her rose-tinted lips in a silent kiss.

Jason threw back his head and laughed uproariously.

"Lord, Edith, you're incorrigible," he told her good-humoredly. "You've been working for me for more than ten years, and I still never know what to expect of you! You're wicked, Edith. Wicked."

"Variety is the spice of life, remember. I am what I am. When I married your best friend, you weren't too happy about it, as I recall. Your exact words, and I quote, 'John is straight as an arrow—he is undoubtedly the most predictable person I know. He doesn't drink, smoke or chase women. Lord, the man doesn't even cuss! John Ward should've been a preacher.

" 'I can't see it, Edith. Not you and John. At times you are brazen beyond belief, on occasion you've made even *me* blush. You are brash, impulsive, unpredictable, and one never knows what you might do. The only thing John can expect is the unexpected.' End of quote.''

"And I was right on the mark, wasn't I?''

She dissolved into gales of laughter, and Jason joined in, for the moment forgetting his problems and troubles.

Edith Banning Ward was a ray of sunshine in her brother's life. She was only two years his junior, and they had grown up together and been extremely close. They had experienced all the childhood illnesses at the same time, had shared their teenage escapades and had even double-dated most of the time.

She was beautiful, with a keen sense of humor, a great personality and a head for business that she, by choice, didn't use. When the Banning fortune had reverted to the heirs, Edith had simply turned her share over to her big brother, saying, "Jason has the business sense in the family.''

Their young sister, Kendra had followed Edith's lead. Her reason, however, was that she simply didn't want to be bothered. So long as Jason looked out for her in a financial way, it didn't matter to her how it came to her.

The maverick of the Banning family, Kendra was the unexpected product of her parents' love of almost twenty-one years. Born to the union late in her parents' lives, she had been pampered outrageously. And she had grown into a beautiful, strong-willed young woman. Jason never knew when he'd hear from her or where she might be when he did. But the three remaining Bannings loved each other dearly, and Kendra's carefree nature was tolerated and excused by the other two.

In the past few years, rather than taking the role of his little sister, Edith had become a mother hen, clucking about Jason's long work hours, the fact that he didn't eat properly and didn't get enough rest. Of course, his "love life" or rather, the lack of one, was a sore point, as well.

Jason had discussed his feelings for Corey with Edith, and had gone into great detail about Corey's unreasonable dislike and mistrust of him. He had been surprised to learn that Edith had been fully aware of his secret attraction. She had known about Corey Kelton since the day Jason had returned home frustrated, not because a certain young lady had rammed her car into his new Mercedes, but because that young lady was such a very young lady!

When asked how she had known about Corey, Edith had given him a smug, knowing grin and replied simply, "Walls have ears." Which meant that she had been listening outside the study that day when Jason had reported the story to their father. He had even gone so far then as to admit to his "ridiculous and impossible" attraction for the young Kelton beauty: "A sixteen-year-old, for Christ's sake!" An attraction that had turned into an obsession.

"Jason? Yoo-hoo, Ja-son." Edith waved her hand before her brother's face to regain his attention, so lost in thought was he. "Medic! Medic!" she yelled exaggeratedly when she didn't receive an immediate response.

"Huh? Oh, Edith. Where were we?"

"We were discussing John becoming a preacher," she informed him in a very serious manner, then burst out laughing at the blank look on Jason's face. "But I'm sure that's not why you called me in here. So start being a boss and give me some orders."

"Yes, well," he murmured, then continued, "I've done a lot of thinking, Edith, and I'm thinking of offering Cappy and Corey the money they gave Matt Fielder with the mistaken idea that it was to salvage the studios. What do you think about the idea?''

Immediately Edith suspected this to be an attempt to bridge the gap between Corey and him. She felt he needed her support and approval in his decision and thought seriously for a moment before giving him her answer.

''It's an extremely generous thing to do, Jason, especially since neither you nor the studio were benefited by their money,'' she began. Then, on a thoughtful note, she went on, ''Of course, it's just like you to want to do it, knowing the circumstances.''

She paused and stood gazing at a spot somewhere above Jason's head, and he waited, knowing full well she had more to say. After a moment she resumed her answer to his question.

''You can make the offer, Jason, and I feel sure that Cappy will not only appreciate the gesture, but I believe he will accept it. But Corey...''

Her words trailed away, and she met Jason's inquiring look. Slowly, wordlessly, she shook her russet head, and worry clouded her green eyes.

''I know,'' Jason agreed. ''I may be adding fuel to her fire, but it's a chance I'm willing to take. At least, if I make an attempt to reimburse her for the loss of her savings, she'll have to admit that I'm trying to do the right thing.''

''And there's always that outside chance that she'll be reasonable about it and understand your intent.'' Edith's words carried no conviction whatsoever, and she ended with a slight shrug of her shoulders.

''Well, it's worth a try,'' Jason returned, running his tanned fingers through his dark hair, a faint frown touching his brow. ''Now that the decision has been made, I'm anxious to get on with it.'' With a glance at his watch he continued, ''They should be just about done with the scene they're shooting and due to take a lunch break. Please ask Cappy and Corey to come to my office immediately afterward.''

''Thanks, Jason!''

Cappy stuffed the check into his wallet, slipped it into his rear pocket and reached out to shake Jason's hand.

''Sure thing, Cappy. And thank you for your willingness to help Matt and your understanding in this whole mess.''

''Well,'' the older man began, ''you weren't obligated to repay the money, Jason. It had nothing to do with Matt's dealings with you, nothing at all. I let Matt have it because of Corey. I was trying to save something that would have been hers one day. Since it didn't turn out that way...'' His half smile and the shrug of his shoulders completed his sentence.

''I understand, my friend, more than you know,'' Jason said, more to himself than to Cappy. ''Do you know if Corey got the message that I want to see her?''

''I'm not sure, but I'll track her down and see that she knows. And, Jason?'' Cappy looked earnestly into the other man's eyes. ''Good luck with Corey.''

''Thanks, I'm sure I'll need it,'' Jason told him.

With a nod of his head, Cappy left the office, closing the door softly behind him.

''One down, one to go,'' Edith chirped, slipping into Jason's office from the smaller adjoining one.

''It's the 'one to go' that's got me worried,'' Jason said truthfully. ''Why is it that I feel as if I'm Goliath about to go up against David?''

''It's David against Goliath, Jason,'' Edith corrected sweetly.

''David won, Edith.''

''Oh!'' was all she said.

* * *

Jason paced the room like a caged animal and glanced at his watch for the umpteenth time. Only five minutes had elapsed since the last time he'd looked.

Fleetingly he wondered again how he could allow himself to be intimidated by Corey Kelton. It wasn't that she awed or frightened him: he just wasn't thrilled about entering into a new skirmish in the running battle between them. A battle in which they would never have engaged except for Matt Fielder's inability to handle his business, his habits and his life.

Cappy had been easy enough, being a reasonable and understanding person. But Corey would be another matter. Corey was— What *was* Corey? Willful, hot-tempered, unreasonable and unforgiving. God, but that little lady could hold a grudge. How would he handle her? Once again he went over in his mind just how to say what must be said. For once in his life Jason Banning was unsure of himself.

And some ten minutes later when Corey knocked on his door, Jason still wasn't prepared.

"Come in!" Jason called out, his voice loud to his own ears. Nerves, he thought in self-disgust. Irritated at his feeling of inadequacy, he drew a deep breath and braced himself for the pending confrontation.

Unknowingly, Jason held his breath as he watched the door swing open to reveal Corey framed in the doorway. She stood looking at him, defiance in every line of her shapely body.

"You wanted to see me?" she asked without preamble, her voice edged with caution and laced with suspicion. Making no move to enter the room, she waited for Jason's reply, her small form rigid as she studied him with wariness in her tawny eyes.

"Come in and sit down, Corey," Jason instructed, indicating the chair before his desk with a curt nod of his head.

"Look, Jason, can this wait? I'm due back for a shoot, and Cappy—"

"Cappy is prepared to shoot around you," he broke in evenly. With an outward calm that belied the upheaval within him, Jason perched on the corner of his desk, swinging one foot lazily back and forth.

"And I am waiting to talk with you," he said pointedly when Corey remained obstinately poised in the open doorway. "You're pitting strength against strength, Corey, and it isn't necessary," Jason admonished, pinning her with his gaze. "Come in, close the door and sit down," he told her patiently, then added, "please."

With a sigh, whether of resignation, weariness or defeat, Jason would not attempt to guess, Corey moved into the room and sat gingerly on the edge of the chair. Her demeanor screamed resistance to anything he had to say and, as always, where Jason was concerned, she was prepared to be defensive.

There was a heavy silence as their eyes met and each mentally measured the other.

"I'll come right to the point," Jason began. Skewing around to reach across the desk, he pulled open a drawer, withdrew his checkbook and began writing as he talked. "You and I will never see eye to eye regarding the rights or the wrongs of my taking over Fielder Studios. You see, Corey, you, Cappy, me, we're all victims—"

"You?"

"Yes, me!" Jason returned curtly. "But we've been over all this before, and no matter what I do or say, no matter how hard I try or how much proof you've been given, you refuse to let go. So…" His words trailed away as he scrawled his name at the bottom of the check and stared down at the paper unseeingly. "After this film is completed, Banning Productions is releasing you from your contract. You'll be free. No more Banning-Kelton skirmishes."

Corey sat back in her chair and stared at Jason, conflicting thoughts whirling through her head. The movie was very near completion, so this meant that very soon she'd be free of Jason and her contract. So why didn't she feel excitement about it? Why didn't she feel that sense of relief she'd expected? Why did it seem as if he had just knocked the wind from her? And, more important at the moment, why did she feel an unreasonable anger rapidly building up?

She shook her head and forced herself to listen to Jason, realizing that he had been speaking while she had been thinking, and knowing that she had missed much of what he'd said.

"...so Cappy accepted the reimbursement of his money, and it is my intent to repay you, as well," Jason was saying as he leaned forward and handed the check to her.

With trembling fingers Corey took the slip of paper and scanned it, noting that the sum was more than she had lent Matt. Slowly she shook her head and lifted her eyes to meet Jason's anxious gaze.

"I know—" Jason began.

Suddenly she sprang from her chair and stood staring. Her nostrils flared, her mouth was drawn into a thin, straight line, and her eyes burned with unshed tears. Her furious gaze never wavering, with slow deliberation she began to tear the check into tiny pieces, then threw them straight into his astonished face.

"I don't want your blood money, Mr. Banning!" Corey said from between clenched teeth, her breast rising and falling with the intensity of her emotions.

"Damn you, Corey! What in hell will it take?" Jason exploded, his face flushed with anger, his fists clenched at his sides. "Why can't you be reasonable? Blood money! That's what you—" His words broke off, and he continued in a quieter voice. "I made Cappy the same offer, and he accepted it graciously. He didn't resort to name-calling; he took it with the same spirit with which it was extended. He understands—"

"Fine!" she broke in. "I'm glad *he* understands because *I* sure as hell don't. You can keep your conscience money! I'm not going to help you salve your conscience by taking money to assuage your feeling of guilt."

"Guilt?" Jason repeated angrily. "I'm not guilty of anything, and I'm fed up with you, lady!" he roared, slamming his fist down on the desktop with a force that caused papers to scatter. "Up to here," he added, making a cutting motion in his neck with the flat of his hand. "I'm sick and tired of your ridiculous attitude, Miss Kelton. And let me tell you something else—you've pushed me as far as you're going to. Have you got that?

"Jason Banning was there, a prime target for Corey Kelton's frustrations and anger. Anger at the world because of problems too big for you to handle. Anger because you feel that fate has been unkind to you. And I've received the brunt of your anger. I've been your whipping post. I've felt the sting of your hurt. Why? Because I, too, tried to help out a friend. Because I was stupid enough to make a business deal with a known gambler and a drunk. And you're damned lucky I did! Otherwise, you and a lot of others in this studio would be knocking on doors, trying to find a job, trying for a contract with another production company. You should be grateful that I was there when Matt Fielder so ungracefully bowed out."

Silence fell over the room. Tawny eyes locked with emerald ones in silent combat, and the two stood unmoving for several moments.

"You were the one who demanded that I remain under contract with this studio. I wasn't given a choice. Remember that!" Corey defended with renewed spirit. "I wanted no part of you nor your—"

"You damned well don't have to worry about *that* any-more, because I don't want any part of you, either!" Jason countered, contempt ringing in his voice.

For a stunned moment Corey stared wordlessly at the irate man, not at all pleased with his words. It was all right for her to fling hateful words at him, she thought. She'd certainly done it plenty of times before. But she hadn't expected him to reply in kind.

"Damn! Why do I even try?" Jason's words were hushed and threaded with irony. His shoulders slumped wearily, and he slowly walked around the desk to drop heavily into his chair. With a deep, ragged sigh, he leaned his elbows on the desk and hid his face in his hands.

"Go away, Corey," came Jason's muffled order.

The utter weariness in his voice wrung her heart. Corey felt a sudden urge to cradle that dark head against her bosom and made to move toward him, but her better judgment cautioned her. She stood uncertainly, a battle raging on the inside. She had never seen Jason look so...what? Defeated? No, a man like Jason would never succumb to defeat. It was his nature to fight—to win. Yet there he sat, looking so very alone, so tired, so vulnerable.

What had happened to her resolution to face the truth? Corey wondered. Her resolve to face herself and the world? Had she only been fooling herself? Why had she reacted as she had to Jason's attempt to repay her?

Yes, one part of her was still loyal to Matt and his mem-ory, too stubborn to give in. The other part of her truly be-lieved in Jason and the sincerity with which he had tried to right what he considered a wrong done to Cappy and her. And she had taken offense, had stormed at him in anger and had thrown the shredded pieces of his check in his face.

Again she felt the unreasonable need to reach out, to touch him. God, she wanted to tell him she was tired of feeling anger, tired of the hurt, the confusion. She wanted to tell Jason that she, too, was weary of fighting. Fighting with him, fighting her desire for him and fighting her conflicting emotions.

Corey wanted him to know that she had faced up to so many things she hadn't understood, that so much had fallen into place, that she had thought she was ready to face herself, Jason and the world, head-on!

But when the time had come to face Jason—well, so much for facing that problem!

After an endless time, Jason looked up. There was no expression on his impassive face, no sign of emotion. A pain cut through her, piercing her heart with a searing intensity. A small cry sounded in her throat, and she reached out, her fingers brushing his temple.

Jason jerked as if he'd been touched by a live wire, his breath caught harshly, loudly, and his eyes blazed. "Don't touch me!" he rasped out.

"Jason—"

"Get out of here, Corey!" The words were spoken quietly as he rose from his desk, jamming his hands into the pockets of his jeans. "Get out while I have the strength to let you go."

Without a word, Corey left the room.

Nine

Jason stood in the shadows of the large studio, watching the shoot in progress. Mentally following the script, Jason watched it unfold in the scene being played before him. His roving gaze rested on Corey, and a wistful smile touched his lips.

In the role of Judith, Corey paced restlessly about her bedchamber, explaining to her loyal maid the plot she had concocted to trap her unfaithful husband in his infidelity.

Like Corey, Judith had a closed mind, ready and willing to believe only the worst of the poor man who was totally innocent of any of the offenses of which he had been accused. His only guilt was that of loving Corey—no, Judith, Jason corrected himself.

Lord, he was having a hard time separating fiction from real life. He remembered back to the day only a week past when Corey had deviated from the script.

He had been stunned when Corey had whispered his own name during the scene and had held him spellbound by the flames of passion burning in her tawny eyes. When she had touched her lips to his, and the flame sparked— It was incredible! No woman should be able to kiss like that if she didn't mean it. No woman should be able to wreak such havoc on a man. Why had she kissed him? Why had she taken that step?

Then later there had been that awful scene in his office. Jason quickly cleared his mind of that incident; it truly wasn't one he wished to remember. There were sweeter memories tucked away in his heart, sweeter memories in his mind to recall: like the feel of her body along his, her soft, throaty whimpers, the taste of her. He would never forget the husky sound of her voice when she whispered his name, never forget the raw desire that burned in her eyes.

"Cut!"

Cappy's loud voice heavy with frustration, brought Jason abruptly back from his mental wandering. Not knowing the problem, he watched in bewilderment as Cappy stormed across the set, then smiled as the older man approached a red-faced prop man and asked in a heated tone why there was a wristwatch on the table when the time period of the movie was the 1700s!

Jason chuckled to himself and shook his head. Glancing at his own watch, he turned and left the room, but not before his gaze sought and rested once more on Corey.

The door burst open with a loud bang, and Jason looked up inquiringly from the stack of file folders he was sifting through.

"Oh, Jason!" Edith fluttered, her voice high-pitched with excitement. "Look!"

She crossed the room, carelessly shoved a pile of papers aside, perched herself on Jason's desk and unceremoniously plopped her treasure atop the folder in front of him.

"What is it?" Jason questioned staring at the dusty metal box as if it were an alien object.

"For Pete's sake, Jason, what does it look like?" Edith sputtered impatiently.

"A metal box," he replied, smiling indulgently.

"Right! And what do people put in locked metal boxes?"

"You tell me."

"Money! Bonds! Jewelry!" she exclaimed, waving her hands in the air.

Jason didn't appear to be as intrigued by the box and its possible contents as she thought he would be, and Edith jumped from her perch. Her hands on her slim hips, she watched her brother examine the box with indifference.

"Well?" she prodded.

"Well, what?"

"Open it, Jason!" she urged, her curiosity getting the better of her patience.

"I can't."

"Why not?" Edith fairly shouted.

"It's locked, that's why not," Jason informed his wide-eyed sister, an impish grin on his full lips as he pushed the metal container aside as if it was of little or no consequence.

"Ooh, you're impossible, Jason Banning!"

Jason watched in amusement as Edith snatched up and studied the object of their discussion with narrowed green eyes. "It shouldn't be that difficult," she said, as if to herself. Then, to Jason, "It's a small lock. Do you have a screwdriver?"

"Nope."

"How about a nail file?"

"Sorry."

"A hairpin?"

"Excuse me?"

The look on Jason's face was priceless, and Edith laughed aloud. "A letter opener? Surely you've got a letter opener!"

"That I do have," Jason agreed.

He reached into the middle desk drawer and retrieved the opener but didn't hand it over. Instead he leaned back in his chair, stretched out his long legs to rest his feet upon the desk and sat gently slapping the small blade across his open palm.

"It isn't our box, you know. Maybe we shouldn't open it."

"Pooh!" Edith returned fervently.

"'Pooh'?" Jason erupted into a peal of laughter. "'Pooh'?" Again his deep laughter rang out.

"Oh, Jason, shut up!" Edith demanded good-naturedly. "You own this building and its contents. The box was found on the premises, which belong to Banning Productions. So! That means it belongs to us," she ended triumphantly.

"I tried to warn her, Your Honor," Jason exclaimed dramatically. "But you know women, sir—there's just no stoppin' 'em."

"Come on, Jason, *please*," Edith cajoled. She always could get to him and always got just what she wanted. His little sister had him wrapped around her little finger. Always had, always would.

Edith's curiosity finally communicated itself to him, and Jason handed her the letter opener. After several attempts to jimmy the lock without success, she wordlessly shoved the box and letter opener across the desk, and Jason tried his hand.

When the lock finally gave way, Jason lifted his eyes to his anxiously waiting sister with an affirmative nod of his dark head, and Edith gave a small cry of victory.

Jason lifted the lid and saw that the box was crammed with a hodgepodge of papers, all stuffed in haphazardly.

Hanging over his shoulder, Edith sighed with disappointment. "Gee, I thought maybe there would be jewels or something valuable. At least *something* interesting hidden in it. Why would anyone be eccentric enough to lock up such a jumble of crumpled papers? Any chance there might be a mystery key—" she was saying hopefully when Jason broke in.

"What a romantic you are," Jason told her, teasingly. "Always looking for intrigue. Well, who knows? There might be an old love letter stashed in here. There might still be hope," he told her encouragingly. "Tell you what! I'll go through everything and let you know if I find anything interesting. How's that?"

With a shrug of her trim shoulders, Edith turned away and set about closing the boxes on the floor and sealing them with wide paper tape, her disappointment apparent.

Actor that he was, Jason managed to hide his mounting excitement at the prospect of what the metal case might reveal and wondered what had been important enough for Matt to lock away. Not wishing to rekindle Edith's interest in the mysterious container, he casually pushed it aside and resumed the work he had been doing before the interruption, awaiting a time when he could be alone to examine the papers at his leisure.

The long day had finally ended. Shooting for the day had ceased, cameras had rolled to a stop, and the cast had dispersed. The stagehands had cleared the stage, set up for scenes to be filmed the next day and gone home.

Edith had dropped a kiss on her brother's brow and departed, leaving Jason alone in the darkened building, the only light burning in his own office.

Eagerly Jason pulled the cryptic box across the desk and lifted the lid. But for a moment he simply sat staring at the disorderly heap of papers that threatened to spill out and wondered anew what Matt had considered of such great significance that it warranted being locked up and hidden away on the back of a storage room shelf where Edith had found it.

With a feeling of pending discovery, Jason took out the first folded paper and scanned it: it was an outdated lease on the building. One after another, the papers revealed little of any consequence. Mixed in with them there were a few snapshots, the subjects of which had been Griff and Livia Kelton, Matt Fielder with one or both the Keltons, some of the young couple and a baby, others of them with a small girl. Of course the baby and the small girl were Corey, and Jason looked hard at them, trying to imagine Corey as she had been then.

Sprinkled throughout the contents of the box were letters written by Corey while she had been away at school. Feeling no compunction, Jason read the youthful letters, and the loneliness spelled out on yellowed pages tore at his heart. Then, at her mention of a handsome young male admirer, he felt a tightening in his chest, and when he found the snapshot that she had enclosed with the letter, it revealed an obviously happy young Corey and a dashing young man. An unreasonable jealousy surged through Jason. He turned the picture over and read the date scrawled on the back. Corey would have been about eighteen at the time.

Nearing the bottom of the box, Jason found a small gold locket. He picked it up and examined it. "Sweet Sixteen" was engraved in beautiful script on the front of the heart-shaped cover, and a trail of small diamonds graced one side of the heart. Turning it over, he read the inscription on the back cover: "Eternal Love." Beneath those words was inscribed "Mother and Daddy." Inside the locket was a small photo of her parents and, on the opposite side, one of Corey at sixteen—as Jason remembered her from the day of the minor automobile collision the day Jason Banning had lost his heart to her.

Looking more closely, he discovered that the clasp of the locket was broken. Corey probably thought the beloved trinket from her parents had long been lost, he mused.

On a sudden impulse, Jason dropped the locket into his shirt pocket over his heart. It made him feel somehow closer to Corey, and he decided to have the clasp repaired, the locket cleaned and polished. Then his thoughts ran on: he would have it gift-wrapped and present it to her. Perhaps the thoughtful gesture would let her know that Jason Banning was human, after all.

Returning his attention to the box, he found only a couple more unimportant papers and an odd assortment of items. An old penny, a pair of inexpensive cuff links, a tie tack with the chain broken off, a few buttons and a safety pin.

Leaning back in his chair, Jason surveyed the small stack of papers that he had unfolded, uncrumpled and straightened out. Not much reason to lock up and hide what he had found, he thought wearily.

He reached for a file folder, placed all the documents in it and snapped a large rubber band lengthwise about it and another crosswise ensuring that nothing would be lost from it.

Pushing back his chair, he leaned forward to open the large file drawer of his desk and spied a single sheet of paper lying on the floor, almost beneath his feet. It must have fallen off the small untidy mound of papers he had removed from the box and landed on the floor unnoticed.

Picking up the sheet, he glanced quickly over the contents. He had only read a few lines before he sat bolt upright, his body tense, his green eyes wide and staring.

It was a legitimate, duly notarized written agreement between Griffin Kelton and Matthew Fielder, setting forth the conditions of the joint venture of the two. A joint venture to be called "Fielder Studios."

As Jason read, he realized that Griff Kelton had put up the bulk of the capital for the venture, that Matt had, in fact, contributed little, in a monetary sense, as his main involvement was to be the management of the enterprise. A successful producer and director with other, more important interests that claimed priority, Griff had chosen to remain anonymous, a silent partner in the endeavor. The bottom line of the agreement stated that Fielder Studios would become the property of Corey Kelton upon the demise of the principal owners—both of whom were now deceased.

Corey Kelton was unquestionably the rightful owner of Fielder Studios! What a nice kettle of fish Jason Banning had gotten himself into. Why hadn't he had all this checked out when Matt had come to him for financial help? Surely there was a legal record of a transaction of such magnitude as this one. Very successful in the past, Fielder Studios had been around for a long time, and it had been commonly accepted throughout the film industry that Matt owned it.

Well, Jason wondered in genuine perplexity, where do we go from here?

Ten

Are we talking about the same Jason Banning?'' Cappy's question boomed out, surprise lighting his eyes, his mouth agape.

"The very same," Corey assured him quietly. "And please lower your voice, people are looking at us," she advised, looking around the crowded restaurant.

"Damned if miracles don't still happen!" He shook his head wonderingly and took a sip of his coffee before meeting Corey's troubled gaze. He watched her tighten her grip about her cup and stare down into the black depths of her coffee. "Let me get this straight," he began slowly. "You think you're in love with Jason, but you don't want to be, because now it matters to you but not to him. When you weren't in love with him, you believed he wanted you and you didn't care, but now you care about him and he doesn't care about you, and now it matters, but it's too late," he finished in a rush. "Did I get that right?"

"Yes."

"Then, would you mind explaining to me whatever it was that I got right?"

"Oh, Cappy, it's all so confusing."

"I don't doubt that for a minute," Cappy mumbled.

"It's also a long story."

"I've got time, honey," he said gently, encouraging Corey to go on. She needed someone to talk to, someone to share the confusion with. If nothing else, Cappy thought, she could hear herself talk out the problem. He knew that often when a person voiced their fears and heard the words aloud, they could better understand them and were more able to cope.

With a sigh, Corey pushed her coffee away and leaned back against the leather-covered seat in the booth where they sat and closed her eyes for a long moment.

Cappy waited silently and patiently, knowing that she needed the time to put her thoughts together. He had been her friend and confidant for a long time, and he knew her well enough to know that if she'd ever needed a friend, she needed one now.

When Corey opened her eyes again, a faraway look veiled them. She began relating her story, beginning with that day some seven years before when she had first met Jason Banning.

Cappy listened attentively interrupting only to ask a question now and then in order to clarify, in his own mind, the situation she was explaining. All her anguish, grief and heartbreak at the loss of her parents rolled out, her voice choking with the painful memory. She poured out her loneliness of the following years. She told him how often her thoughts had turned to the handsome young Jason and how that, when she was eighteen, she had attempted to find out where he was on location in Mexico. And how Matt had repeatedly hindered her efforts, thwarting her at every turn.

So Matt had been aware of Corey's attraction to Banning, Cappy mused and realized that the fact angered him. Cappy had always been aware of the attraction between the two. The sparks had flew between them—a blind man may not have been able to see it, but he sure would have felt them! And if it hadn't been for Matt's interference, Corey and Jason might have been together years ago. Matt Fielder had cheated Corey again!

"Did you ever try to locate Jason any more?" Cappy inquired, feeling he knew the answer.

"Yes," Corey answered sadly. "I'd gone to dinner with a few friends, and we ended up at the studio. We ran into Shea English, she was there to preview *Heart's Desire*, a film in which she had co-starred . . ." Her voice trailed off.

"And Jason was the male lead in that film," Cappy finished.

"Watching him on the screen that night awoke all the yearnings that had been deep inside me since I was sixteen. It was awful, Cappy. I felt such jealousy toward Shea, all the times she was held in his arms, every kiss they shared, every tender word he spoke to her.

"It was a movie, for heaven's sake! They were only playing a part, but it didn't seem that way. Then Shea would make a remark about Jason, about how difficult it was to keep her mind on acting when he touched her, how one could get lost in his eyes and that not all those steamy kisses were for the screen.

"It was absolutely miserable, and I left before the film was over. I cried myself to sleep, not only that night, but many nights afterward. A few months later I asked Matt about Jason, and he told me he was somewhere in England, 'off filming his next "award-winning" lust film.' Then he added—and I'll never forget his words—'I wonder how long the "great heartthrob" will last when his adoring female audience finds out about his marriage to that little groupie he knocked up.' Needless to say, I went on another crying marathon.''

"I never heard anything about Jason getting married," Cappy interpolated. "If he did, and mind you, I said *if* he did, it has certainly been a well-kept secret!"

"It wasn't a secret, Cappy. It never happened! Matt lied to me about Jason. He was 'protecting me,' he said. Banning wasn't the kind of man he wanted to see me get involved with. He told me that Jason would use me and toss me aside when he tired of playing with me."

"And in your love for Matt, in your trust—"

"I forgave him for lying to me because it was for my own good. And I tried to force myself to forget my childish dreams of loving and being loved by Jason."

"But you didn't forget Jason, did you, Corey?" Cappy asked gently. He reached across the table to clasp her small hand in his own and hold it firmly, comfortingly.

"No," she whispered. "No, I didn't forget."

"That's enough!" Jason panted, coming up from all-fours to his knees. "Uncle Jay's getting a bit old for this roughhousing."

Playfully he punched at his ruddy-faced five-year-old nephew, who wasn't ready to give up the game.

"Aw, but—" the youngster wailed.

"No buts, Evan Ward," Edith put in. "Besides, it's nearly time for dinner. Get yourself to the bathroom and wash up."

When the child had left the room, Jason got to his feet and made his way to the sofa, wiping his perspiring brow with the back of his hand. "Not as young as I used to be," he commented with a laugh.

"That isn't it at all, Jason Banning!" Edith told him wisely. "I watched you two romping, and you certainly haven't aged that much since last weekend! Come on 'fess up. Your heart just wasn't in it, right?''

Jason turned tired eyes on his sister. "Right! And you're responsible for it—you and your damned, mysterious metal box.''

"Oh. So I have to take the blame for it, do I?'' she returned with her usual good humor. "Would the situation be any different if I hadn't found the box? Incidentally, she doesn't know about it, does she?''

"I haven't told her anything yet,'' he said heavily, rising to pace to the window. He stood looking out for a few minutes, then turned back to Edith with a rueful laugh. "Our relationship isn't on the best footing at this moment. I'm not sure how she'll react when I show her the agreement between her father and Matt. It will come as a shock to learn that her father not only had financed Fielder Studios originally, but that she's been a partner for the past seven years—both facts that Matt deliberately chose to withhold from her. Damn!'' Jason swore loudly. "I should have had John do a more thorough check on Matt Fielder.''

As if the mention of his name had conjured him up, John Ward entered the room and laid his briefcase on a nearby chair. Shrugging out of his coat, he crossed the room, greeted Edith with a kiss and turned to Jason.

"I heard what you were saying, Jason, and you're right,'' he spoke hurriedly. "We just didn't delve deeply enough into Fielder's affairs. After you called me about the agreement you found, I made some calls and did some investigating.''

"And?'' Jason prompted, his questioning eyes following John's movements as the other man retrieved his briefcase, sat down and opened it to draw out some papers.

"And that document you found is legal,'' John stated, adding, "in a sense.''

"What do you mean 'in a sense'? Either it is or it isn't," Edith voiced impatiently, perching on the arm of her husband's chair.

"Depends on how one looks at it. You see, Griff Kelton trusted Matt and allowed him to put everything in his own name, knowing that Matt couldn't do anything without Griff's approval—approval being in the form of finances, major decisions such as additions, alterations, contracts, et cetera. To all outward appearances, Matt was the owner of the studio. For reasons of his own, Griff requested that he be a silent partner, which is legal and often done.

"I think he was making an all-out effort to help his best friend to make something of himself, to create a self-image, to command respect from a lot of his colleagues who knew his weaknesses and had no faith in him. A selfless, generous act, if you ask me. Griff Kelton must have been quite a man."

Jason listened carefully, thoughtfully, and felt that he could understand Griff's reasoning.

"John, are you saying that the studio doesn't belong to Jason? That it belongs to Corey?" Edith asked in dismay, her green eyes resting on her brother.

"As her father's beneficiary, Corey owned a half interest, even before Matt died, Edith," John pointed out. "That means she was liable for half of the debts, liable for half the loan Jason extended. Upon Matt's death, had the situation been different, she would have been the sole owner. But due to Matt's deceit and his agreement with Jason—"

"Oh, my God!" Jason's exclamation caught both John's and Edith's attention.

"I see you're piecing it all together, Jason, and that you already realize what I was about to say," John stated quietly.

"What?" Edith demanded, standing from the chair. "What?"

"If Jason should choose to do so, he could call in all monies owed him by Fielder Studios, and Miss Kelton would be responsible for the debt because, according to the original agreement, she became sole owner at Fielder's death!

"The agreement between Matt and Jason is legal and binding. However, it pertains to Matt's half interest *only*. Fielder could not dispose of property belonging to another, nor could he use that portion as collateral without the approval of that party."

"So, what you're saying is that Corey owns half of the studios and Jason owns the other?" Edith asked slowly.

"At the moment, yes," came John's reply. Then he asked, "Jason, is Miss Kelton in the financial situation to repay the loan you extended?"

"No. Corey doesn't have that kind of money."

"If she could repay and if Jason accepted the payment, Miss Kelton would be sole owner. Since she cannot, she and Jason are equal partners in the enterprise," John stated, replacing the papers in his case. "That technicality must be handled properly. Meaning, legally! We will have to draw up papers to that effect, and I can have them ready within a week."

Silence hung in the room, each lost in his own thoughts. Then Jason stood, walked across the room to the wet bar and poured a stiff drink.

"As your legal advisor, I can be the one to explain to Miss Kelton about these developments, Jason," John offered.

"No, it had best come from me," Jason said heavily, tossing down the Scotch. "Thanks for offering."

Going to her brother's side, Edith laid a comforting hand on his arm. "You needn't be the one to tell her, Jason," she said softly, her lovely face filled with compassion. She knew how difficult it would be for him. "Why not let John—"

"I have to do it, Edith. Corey and I are in this thing to-gether. It's my place to tell her that and to explain the hows and the whys."

"When are you going to tell her?" John and Edith asked in unison.

But Jason didn't answer.

Eleven

———

Corey stood at the top of the long staircase, her gaze scanning the room below. From where she stood, she could see the guests as they arrived through the large foyer, as well as had a good view of the oversize living room.

She hadn't wanted to attend this party, but Mario Venetia wasn't a man to turn down. He was one of the film industry's "golden boys," a man with money, influence and prestige. Not only was Venetia coproducer of the film in which Corey was presently working but was *the* producer of *Rainbow Rider*, a highly acclaimed project that was soon to be cast.

Cappy had been chosen to direct *Rainbow Rider*, and Corey wanted badly to land a major role in the film. Cappy had convinced her that she should come to the party. She recalled his words: *"You should be seen. It's good public relations."* Then he had added, *"You might even get a chance to see Jason, and with the two of you on neutral ground. Well, just maybe, you can call a truce. Who knows what might happen?''*

Well, she was here, she thought, she was a nervous wreck, she felt sick to her stomach, and she wanted to go home!

Scanning the room once again, her eyes met Cappy's. He smiled encouragingly, lifted his drink in a silent salute and winked. Corey returned his smile.

"I don't see him," she mouthed the words.

Cappy frowned and craned his neck, searching through the crowd. Directing his attention back to Corey, he shrugged his shoulders, an indication that he hadn't seen Jason among the throng of people.

Once more Corey searched the room, her gaze moving from face to face. There was only one person she sought, one face she hoped to see. She assured herself that tonight she would tell Jason she didn't want to fight anymore, that she did not wish to be free of her contract. What she wouldn't mention was that she had no wish to be free of him!

Yes, tonight was important for many reasons. She would prove to the world, or at least to Cappy, her friends, herself and, hopefully, to Jason that she, Corey Kelton, was strong, that she had decided to face whatever might come her way. That she was tired of running, tired of hiding.

Then she saw him. He stood by the fireplace, one hand thrust into his pocket, the other resting on the mantel. Jason was dressed in a black tux that fit him beautifully, accenting his sensuous body. His rich dark brown hair was slightly mussed, giving him a rakish devil-may-care appearance, and his emerald eyes sparkled as he laughed deeply. Corey's heart beat wildly. How handsome he was! He literally took her breath away.

Turning to the wall mirror behind her on the landing, Corey looked appraisingly at the image the glass reflected. Assuring herself that her hair and makeup were satisfactory, Corey descended the stairs and entered the noisy, crowded living room.

Jason had been chatting with a small group of men, but his attention was drawn to the vision of beauty coming down the stairs to join the party guests. His gaze swept over her, hungrily taking in every detail of her slender form.

The pale blue silk evening gown, shot with threads of sapphire and gold, caressed her lush curves almost like a second skin. Tiny straps of a darker blue ran over her smooth tanned shoulders and crossed over the low-plunging back. The high slit on the side afforded a tantalizing view of her shapely leg. From a single gold chain encircling her slender neck, hung a small cluster of sapphires cradling a lone diamond that rested lightly above the soft curve of her full breast. Her honey-brown hair was swept upward and gathered with a satin ribbon, and tiny whispers of curls framed her lovely face.

Anyone watching Jason could have read the unadulterated adoration on his face and recognize the undisguised yearning shining in his emerald eyes.

"Your heart's in your eyes, Jason," Edith whispered in her brother's ear.

"Hello, little sister," Jason greeted, momentarily distracted. Turning to her, he dropped a kiss on Edith's cheek. "John—" his nod acknowledged his brother-in-law "—I didn't see you two arrive."

"Your attention was otherwise engaged," John returned, his voice laced with amusement.

Corey had been claimed by Anita Venetia, who was talking nonstop about her husband's next adventure. Corey knew that it would be wise to be friendly and congenial to Mario's wife: their friendship might help pave the way to landing the role in *Rainbow Rider* that she so desired. But she found it increasingly difficult to stand listening to the woman, with an artificial smile pasted on her lips, when her mind was on Jason.

Glancing up, Corey met Jason's stare. The intensity of his heated gaze was like a tangible thing and seemed to sear her very soul. There was an almost magnetic pull, beckoning her to him.

When Jason inclined his head in silent acknowledgment and gave her a heart-wrenching smile, Corey tilted her head and returned it with a brilliant smile. She watched the play of emotions on his handsome face with interest. Apparently he hadn't expected her to respond the way she had. Doubtless he was remembering how she had reacted to his attempt to make amends by offering the reimbursement of her money.

Corey was relieved when a waiter broke in on Anita's monologue with a murmured "Excuse me, madam, but Mr. Venetia asked me to find you and let you know he wishes your presence." With a hurried "Sorry, darling, see you later" and the flutter of her hand Anita was off, and Corey was left standing alone.

Making her way through the multitude of guests, Corey could feel Jason's gaze following her across the room. She felt a warmth well up within her. So he wasn't unaffected by her! That pleased her immensely and encouraged her to feel that, after all, she might have another chance with him. The thought gave her confidence and suddenly she felt vibrantly alive.

"Cork! Damn me if you aren't more beautiful than ever." The deep, rich timbre of the voice at her ear claimed Corey's attention as strong arms encircled her from behind.

Only one person in the world called her *Cork*.

"Stefan!" she shouted in stunned surprise, whirling around to throw her arms about the man. "I can't believe it. You! Here!"

Stefano Sinclair was an arrestingly handsome man, his Greek-Italian blood ran hot through his veins, mixed with a generation of "hard-nosed Arizona rancher" on his father's side, and the combination was explosive. His thick hair was as black as midnight and shone with a blue-black sheen beneath the bright lights overhead. His stance was regal with an air of command, and his powerfully built, well-toned body spelled healthy male animal. But most women were lost from the moment they gazed into the fathomless depths of his snapping ebony eyes.

Stefan crushed Corey to him, enveloping her in his strong embrace and brushing his lips with a feathery kiss before standing her from him.

"Let me look at you," he ordered, smiling that dimpled smile she remembered so well.

Jason saw the striking man rapidly approaching Corey and wondered fleetingly who he might be. His speculative gaze moved from the stranger to Corey and back again. He watched as the man stepped up behind Corey and whispered something in her ear.

Jason's body stiffened with dislike for the unknown man when he saw Corey's face brighten with pleasure and heard her lilting voice cry out the stranger's name. A shaft of jealousy thrust through his belly like a hot coal when Corey turned and flung herself into the other man's arms and lifted her face and welcomed his kiss.

Running a tanned finger under the collar that threatened to choke him, Jason's breath came raggedly. His eyes flashed fire, his fist clenched, and he stood rigidly as he witnessed the scenario before him.

"Oh, Stefan, I've missed you so!" Corey enthused, staring up at the man she loved like a big brother—the brother she never had.

Her first meeting with Stefan had been accidental. She had been studying theater at Arizona State University and had gone to the campus coffee shop to meet her roommate. When Debbie Sinclair arrived, her arm linked possessively with that of a startlingly handsome man, she introduced him to Corey as her big brother. And from that day forward, he had been Corey's "big brother," as well. An ever-strengthening bond had developed between them, and it had been Stefan on whom she had depended while she had been away from Matt and Cappy.

Stefan had loaned her his strength, given her his shoulder to cry on, his hand to hold on to and had embraced her with the warmth of his friendship.

"I've missed you too." Stefan caressed her cheek between his work-hardened hands. "So, why are you at this overelaborate shindig?"

"Well, you know how we starlets are—party, party, party," she announced dramatically and fluttered her eyelashes. "And Cappy says it's good public relations," she added conspiratorially from behind her hand, causing Stefan to throw back his head and roar with laughter. "And why are you, Stefano Josef Sinclair, at this party and dressed in a tuxedo to boot?"

"Family! All for the family," Stefan informed her with a smile and twitched the tip of her nose with his forefinger. "I hate being gussied up in this monkey-suit, but Uncle Mario insisted."

"Uncle Mario? As in 'Mario Venetia'?" Corey asked in genuine awe.

"One and the same."

Stefan's concentration was divided between Corey and some point behind her, and she wondered what, or who, kept drawing his attention. Breeding and good manners prevented her turning her head.

"If looks could kill," Stefan mumbled.

"What?"

"You know the old saying 'If looks could kill.' Well, I'd be a dead man," he stated bluntly.

"What do you mean?"

"There's a mighty angry man over by the hearth, and he's glaring at me with hatred in his eye," Stefan enlightened a confused Corey.

She didn't *have* to turn around to know it was Jason that Stefan was indicating, but she did. Casually she shifted her body until she met the force of Jason's emerald glare. A rare smile tugged at her lips. "Oh, that's just Jason Banning," Corey told Stefan indifferently.

"So, that's the man himself, huh?" Stefan mused and became thoughtful. "You still in love with him, Cork?"

"What?" Corey stared at him in disbelief. "But how did you ...? I never—"

"You didn't have to tell me. It was there in your eyes, threaded deep in your careful words. You haven't managed to land the love of your life, have you, Cork?"

"No," she whispered feelingly. "We do nothing but fight, Stefan. We're constantly at odds; sometimes it's an out-and-out war. I'm always battling my feelings for Jason, and he ... he's indifferent to me."

When he made no comment, Corey raised her eyes and saw that once again Stefan's attention was on Jason. She tugged at his arm to bring him back to her. "Stefan? Hello?"

He looked down at her then, a wide smile curving his lips, devilment lighting his black eyes.

"Stefan! I can see the wheels turning. What are you—"

"I always wanted to be an actor," he muttered.

"You what? Stefan, what—" Her words broke off, and she stumbled slightly as he suddenly pulled her to him.

"Here he comes," he said under his breath, his lips brushing her temple. "Indifferent, is he? We're on, Cork. Too late to explain the script—ad-lib, sweetheart."

"Hello, Corey." Jason's deep voice was tight with disapproval. His green gaze burned into her before moving on to rest questioningly on the man in whose arms she stood.

"Ah, hello, Jason." Corey swallowed with difficulty and stepped away from the circle of Stefan's arms, her eyes darting from one handsome man to the other. "I don't think you two have met. Jason, Stefano Sinclair. Stefan, Jason Banning."

"A real pleasure, Jason," Stefan said with unfeigned enthusiasm, eagerly extending his hand. "And please call me Stefan."

Jason hesitated, then reached to clasp the outstretched hand in a steely grip. "Stefan, it is!"

Both men smiled, and their eyes glittered in unspoken challenge as they put all their strength into the grip, equally matched in strength. It was a clash of wills, but only the two men involved were aware of the fact. Their gazes met in silent combat, and neither of them gave an inch as each man took the measure of the other. A wordless warning passed between them, and they broke the hand grip at the same time.

Stefan chuckled to himself. Jason was anything but indifferent where Corey was concerned. Their little tug-of-war of strength spoke volumes. Jason had been staking his claim and warning Stefan not to poach on his territory. It was rich! Stefan loved it!

He liked Jason Banning, he decided, liked him a lot. He was going to have a great time helping Corey rope the man she loved. Banning had strength, determination and a touch of arrogance—a winning combination, in Stefan's book. Jason reminded Stefan a great deal of himself.

"Good meeting you, Jason." Stefan smiled, nodded at him in dismissal and reached out to place a possessive arm around Corey. "Now, if you'll excuse us, Corey and I are going to find some dark shadows to slip off into." His voice was threaded with an undercurrent of suggestion. "We've got a lot to talk about, right? And I can't say what I want to say in a roomful of people. I'm sure you understand," he finished on a husky note, winking at Jason.

"Yes," Corey broke in, snuggling closer to Stefan. "Dark shadows seem like a perfect place. Do you suppose we could swipe a bottle of champagne?"

"I've never known you to drink, Corey," he said, looking at her askance.

"I've never felt so daring before," she returned flippantly. "I want to experience *all* the sinful things I've been avoiding. Let's throw caution to the winds!"

Her words floated back to Jason as she and Stefan weaved their way through the crowd of guests and toward the terrace doors. His fury barely restrained, Jason saw Stefan take two glasses from a tray and pluck a bottle of champagne from an ice bucket before the two stepped through the open doors and disappeared into the night.

"I pity the poor soul who has the misfortune to say the wrong thing to Banning," Stefan chuckled as he and Corey walked along the flagstone pathway.

Diamond-bright stars blanketed the black velvet sky, and a full moon drifted in and out of milky clouds. A gentle breeze wafted about the garden, filling the summer night with the heady fragrance of roses.

"It's a beautiful night," Stefan said in an almost reverent tone, gazing at the beauty of the night. "A night for lovers." He looked down at Corey, her face pale and lovely in the moonlight. "You should be out here with a man who would hold you and ignite the fire in your blood with his caress, who would stir your passions with fevered kisses. A man like Jason."

"Yes, like Jason." Corey sighed and stopped at the edge of the large swimming pool, wrapping her arms about her as if she were cold. She stared out across the blue-green water, lost in thought.

Stefan set the glasses and champagne aside and sat down at the pool's edge. Reaching upward for Corey's hand, he tugged her down to sit beside him. They sat for a few minutes in companionable silence.

Then Stefan startled Corey by removing his shoes and socks. She watched, a faint smile on her face, as he rolled up his pants legs and, grinning like a mischievous little boy, plopped his bare feet into the water with a loud splash.

"Join me," he encouraged, running a finger along the strap of her high-heeled sandal.

"It's tempting, but I have stockings on."

"So?" Stefan dared her with his ebony stare. "What happened to your feeling of daring? Experiencing all the sinful things you've been avoiding, throwing caution to the wind?"

"Oh, yeah! I did say that, didn't I," Corey replied with a laugh. After a moment of indecision, she shrugged her shoulders in indifference and said, "Oh, what the heck!" and slipped her sandals from her slender feet.

"Look out, world! Corey Kelton is shedding her inhibitions!" Stefan shouted to the heavens and laughed with childish delight as she put her stockinged feet in the water.

"Do tell!" he said with fake shock. "What sinful thing do you plan to do next?"

"Drink champagne," she announced with spirit, reaching for the bottle and glasses. "And if I had worn slippers instead of sandals, I'd drink the bubbly from my shoe!"

"Omigod!" Stefan pretended to be scandalized and rolled his eyes heavenward. "Dare I hope that after the shocking display of putting your stocking-clad footsies into yon pool, after indulging in drink, that you might also try yet another sinful thing, like ravishing me?"

"One never knows," she quipped and filled the glasses with the sparkling liquid. She handed one glass to her comrade and took a sip of her own, giggling when the fizzing crystal bubbles popped and tickled her nose.

"Cork! Cork, you're incredible," Stefan laughed, sheer amusement dancing in his dark eyes. "Jason's a very lucky man, very lucky. But a fool! Any man would have to be crazy to let you slip through his fingers."

"And a woman would have to be crazy to let a man like you get away," she returned the compliment.

"You know, Cork, you're right!" he agreed, pretending to be serious. "So what do you say! Why don't we two fantastic people get together? Seems the sensible thing to do since we're both such a great catch and neither of us could be considered crazy."

"Oh, no?" she asked playfully. "You can look at us sitting here in evening dress and tux, soaking our feet in the swimming pool and say that?"

"Well, at least I had the sense to remove my socks," he retorted.

With an impish grin, Corey picked up her shoe and threw it across the short distance between them. It met its target, striking Stefan on his broad shoulder, then bounced off, and they watched in stunned silence as the sandal dropped, as if in slow motion, and landed in the swimming pool with a splash. It sank quickly, leaving behind a ripple of small waves.

They turned and stared at each other for a moment, then burst into gales of laughter. The more they laughed, the funnier it was, and before long both had tears coursing down their cheeks.

Stefan reached for his handkerchief and leaned forward to blot Corey's tear-dampened cheeks, then wiped his own. As he did so, he glanced toward the house and saw Jason silhouetted in the terrace doors. How long he had been standing there or how much he had seen, Stefan had no idea, but as he watched, Jason turned and reentered the building.

"Are you still living in Arizona?" Corey asked conversationally, remembering that their visit would be brief and wishing to catch up on what had been happening in the year since she had last seen Stefan.

"You betcha," Stefan replied emphatically. "I'm still raising Arabians. You know that ranching has always been in my blood. Although my ranch is small by some standards, I do have plans for expansion."

"And how's your love life?" she prompted.

"Don't have a love life, but I've got one hell of a night life!" Stefan boasted grandiosely.

"Love 'em and leave 'em, huh?" she asked, a half smile on her face.

"Love doesn't enter into it," he stated with conviction. "I have some good times, but everyone knows the score and knows when to let go and move on."

"It sounds so..." Corey's words trailed off, then she asked, "Stefan, don't you want to fall in love? Don't you want to be loved, I mean *truly* loved?"

"Everyone wants to be loved, Cork, and I'm no exception. But to be honest, I have yet to meet a woman who could make me want to have a serious involvement. Nor do I believe I will *ever* find such a woman. I have a good life, I relish my freedom, and I don't hurt for female companionship. The women I choose for short-term association know the limits from the beginning. I'm straightforward in my relationships—and please note that I said 'relationships.' That's the key word. I make no promises, no commitments, and if the lady accepts those terms, we get along fine," he finished firmly.

"To each his own, I suppose," Corey murmured, lifting her glass to Stefan in silent salute. Then she brought it to her lips and drank it down without pausing. Reaching for the bottle, she poured the last of the champagne into their glasses. She then raised the empty bottle, squinted one eye and peeked into the open neck.

"Hey, kiddo! How many glasses of champagne did we have?"

"Beats me. Don't know, don't care!" she replied with unconcern, touching her glass to his. "A toast!" she trilled. "A toast to love, or in your case, 'relationships.' To friendship, sinfulness, lost inhibitions and throwing caution to the wind!"

"Hear! Hear!" Stefan applauded cheerfully, and they downed the last of the champagne. "Too bad we don't have a fireplace to smash the glasses in," he said regretfully.

"Yeah, too bad!" Corey echoed, her voice a little slurred. "Now how do you s'pose I'm gonna get my shoe back?" She leaned forward, her tawny eyes squinting to focus on the dark object at the bottom of the pool.

"Well," Stefan began, rubbing the back of his hand along his jaw. "We could jump in and get it," he suggested with laughter in his voice.

"Yes!" Corey shouted, springing to her feet. "That's a great idea!"

And with that she pushed an unsuspecting Stefan into the pool, following him with a splash.

Twelve

Jason paced the less crowded end of the room in a temper, avoiding the guests who milled about, sidestepping when a couple danced too near. His face was drawn with anger, and jealousy rose like bile in his throat. Twice he had walked to the door with the intention of leaving the party, yet every time his hand gripped the doorknob, he found himself wishing furiously that it was Sinclair's neck under his hand.

He'd like to have it in a death grip. And when he was finished with him, he'd wring Corey's lovely neck, as well, he fumed.

Edith watched her brother with growing concern as he stood in the doorway looking out into the garden where Corey and that gorgeous man had gone. She chided herself for secretly thinking the man was a handsome devil, somehow feeling disloyal to Jason for doing so.

Poor Jason! Edith thought. Had he waited this long for Corey only to lose her to someone else in the end?

He left the doorway and strode back into the crowded room. Edith saw him stop a passing waiter, pick up a glass of champagne, gulp it down and help himself to another.

Jason was a light drinker, and his action disturbed Edith greatly. Looking across the room, she met the concerned eye of her husband, who had also been watching, worry lining his brow. John's nod told Edith that she should try to intervene, and she moved in Jason's direction.

"You're worrying me, Jason," she told him, laying her hand on his arm lightly. "I've never seen you like this, and it scares me!" Her grip had tightened perceptibly as she spoke. Jason was hurting, and she couldn't help him, and that hurt her.

"What do you think Corey would do if I walked out there and knocked out that pretty-faced Sinclair, tossed her over my shoulder, carried her off and made mad, passionate love to her?" Jason asked with a wicked leer.

Mouth agape, Edith stood staring at him. She didn't answer, hoping that if Jason let off steam to her, perhaps he wouldn't make a scene in the garden.

"Well, what do you think she'd do?" he asked again.

"I-I don't know," she returned hesitantly.

"Sounds like something out of a movie, doesn't it," Jason persisted.

"Ah, yes. Yes, it does," she replied firmly, hoping that he could see how ridiculous such behavior would be.

"It has its possibilities, though," Jason mused aloud. Then he slammed his fist hard against the palm of his hand, making Edith jump. "Yes, the more I think about it . . ."

"Oh, Jason! You wouldn't!" Edith choked out, her eyes wide with disbelief.

"Wouldn't I?" And with those words Jason strode purposefully toward the terrace doors.

John had been watching the exchange between his wife and her brother, and when he saw Jason head for the door, he quickly moved to join Edith, who was making her way toward him, and the two of them resolutely followed Jason.

With deadly intent etched on his handsome face, Jason marched toward the garden. As he neared the pool area, he stopped short at the sound of laughter and splashing water. This was a formal party, a dance, not a swimming party, he thought, momentarily distracted from his purpose as he detoured to the pool, wondering what fools would—

"What the hell!" Jason exploded furiously, his green eyes narrowing dangerously when he recognized the two in the blue-green water.

His resonant voice reached Corey and Stefan, making them start and look up from the pool in surprise.

Hampered by her long skirt, Corey slowly made her way toward shallow water where she could place both feet firmly on the bottom. There she stood waist deep in the water, her very wet, very revealing dress clinging to her, and stared at a Jason Banning she'd never before seen. She could read the unadulterated fury in his eyes. Oh, but he's angry, she thought uneasily.

But the look on his face showed much more than mere anger. Jason Banning was livid! His body fairly trembled with the intensity of his fury, and his lips curled with contempt.

"Uh-oh," Stefan mumbled to the dripping woman as he came to stand beside her. "I'd say our little plan worked. But maybe we overdid it just a tad. What do you think?"

Corey made no reply.

"But didn't we have fun?" Stefan said in an undertone. He was still enjoying their escapade as he gave Jason back glare for glare.

But the fun had gone out of the adventure for Corey.

"H-hello, Jason," she croaked, the word interrupted by a loud, most unladylike hiccup. "Great p-party, isn't it?"

"Corey," he thundered, "you have one very short minute to get out of that pool!" His voice was as hard and cold as steel. He glanced at his watch, as if timing her.

"And if I don't?" she challenged bravely, tilting her chin rebelliously.

"Then I'll come in after you!"

"Did you hear that, Stefan? Jason's going to join us," Corey told her partner in crime. Her dip in the pool hadn't entirely sobered her, and she began giggling. Then she raised her tawny eyes to Jason. "Come on in, the water's fine," she invited.

And to Corey's amazement and horror, Jason walked down the steps and into the water. Slowly, menacingly, he moved steadily toward her.

Mesmerized, Corey made no move to retreat. Her tawny eyes were locked with the unwavering green eyes of the man who was determinedly wading through the water, coming nearer and nearer.

Then Jason reached out and gripped her arm firmly, painfully, and began to retreat from the pool, pulling her after him.

"Let me go!" Corey stormed, struggling to free herself from his iron hold. She thrashed about, splashing water over Jason, who was already soaked up to this thighs. But her efforts to escape his grip were useless, resulting only in the tightening of his hold on her arm.

Looking back over her shoulder, her gaze sought Stefan for support. He stood thigh-high in the water, feet wide apart, arms crossed nonchalantly over his wide chest. There was open amusement in his black eyes, and a wide, toothy grin on his handsome face. At her beseeching look, he dropped his arms to give Corey a thumbs-up sign.

It was her turn to be furious. She was dead! And that lout back there was smiling his fool head off and giving her a damned "all is well" signal! Well, Corey thought with a slight shrug, maybe Stefan was right. Maybe Jason's little walk in the cold water had cooled him off.

She stumbled up the steps as Jason sure-footedly climbed them, still pulling her along behind him. As she reached the last step, he gave her an extra, unnecessary jerk, and she stumbled forward to fall heavily against him as he stopped abruptly on the deck.

Corey stared up at him. Wrong, she thought, he hadn't cooled off. Not in the least. She was definitely a dead person. Never had she encountered such wrath in a person's eyes. How he must despise her, she thought wretchedly.

A sound caused her to glance over, and Corey saw Edith Ward and her husband. Behind them some of the guests had gathered, and whispers and light, smothered laughter reached her ears. They must have witnessed the entire episode! she thought with a groan. Everyone would hear about it, was her next thought. What would Cappy think of her? She bit down hard on her lower lip.

The splashing of water caught her attention, and she turned to see Stefan wading from the pool. He walked up the steps, stopped beside her and shook himself like a dog. Dog! That's what he is, Corey fumed, for getting me into this unholy mess.

"Hey, Jason," Stefan greeted him cheerfully, his voice ringing out. Jason shot him a killing look for his effort. Undaunted, Stefan went on, "No harm done, just old friends having a little fun. You can't blame us for that."

"I blame you, Sinclair, for plying Miss Kelton with champagne and for putting her in an embarrassing situation!" Jason returned coldly.

"But Stefan didn't—"

"Shut up, Corey!" Jason snapped, setting her away from him. "Sinclair should have had some sense, even if *you* didn't!"

"She's a big girl, Banning, in case you haven't noticed. *I* sure as hell have!''

"Why, you—" Jason bit out, and before anyone could react, his fist met Stefan's jaw with a loud crunch, and the man stumbled backward into the pool.

"Stefan!" Corey cried in dismay, running toward the edge. She fell on her knees, her hands reaching out to him. "Oh, Stefan!"

But before his outstretched hand touched hers, Corey was lifted off the ground and flung across Jason's broad shoulder.

"Put me down, Jason Banning!" she screamed, kicking, heedless of the growing audience. "How dare you! Oh, I hate you," she sputtered.

More of the guests had spilled from the house to watch the goings on and, as Jason strode across the yard with his unlikely burden, they moved aside to clear a path for him. Here and there cheers rang out.

"Hey, Banning!" Stefan called to the retreating figure. "Hell of a right you've got, buddy!"

Then, looking about at the stunned faces, Stefan smiled enchantingly, spreading his hands outward in a gesture of total acceptance. "What can I say? I like the guy and, once he gets to know me, he'll like me."

Jason tossed Corey without ceremony into the back seat of the limo and rattled off her address to the driver. Climbing in beside her, he slammed the door. The car pulled smoothly away from the curb.

With a look of utter disgust, Jason wordlessly surveyed the wet, bedraggled woman at his side. From his pocket he extracted one lone shoe and dropped it into her lap. She wondered fleetingly when he had retrieved it from the deck, then remembered that the matching sandal still lay at the bottom of Mario Venetia's pool. That had been their reason for going into the water, she recalled, yet once there, they had forgotten it.

Now, for lack of something to do, Corey leaned down and jammed the sandal on one damp foot. Then she sat in miserable silence. Despite the chill of her wet clothing, she felt hot all over. Moving as far away from Jason as the confines of the car would permit, Corey glared at him.

She wasn't angry that he'd pulled her from the Venetia's swimming pool, nor was she particularly angry that he had made such a scene before all those people. The cause of her real fury was that he had blamed poor Stefan for her being tipsy, and for his lord-and-master attitude when he'd struck her friend. And what *really* burned her up was his display of possessiveness by bodily hauling her away!

The silence lengthened and had become downright unnerving by the time they reached Corey's apartment. The chauffeur opened the door and stood back respectfully as his employer stepped from the car.

Jason reached in, offering a helping hand to Corey. But she merely stared at him belligerently, ignored his hand and slid across the leather seat to step unassisted to the curb.

She heard him dismiss his driver and whirled around.

"It isn't necessary for you to see me to my door, Jason!" she informed him haughtily. "I'll do fine by myself," she finished in a huff and turned to leave, only to be brought to a sudden halt when Jason's hand closed about her upper arm.

Without a word, he escorted her up the steps and into the lobby.

As they passed through, Corey smiled at the shocked young woman who sat behind the desk.

"Good evening, Miss Darcy," she greeted her, as if nothing were amiss.

They had to look a sight, Corey reflected, noting the open stares of the people in the lobby. They were dressed to kill in formal evening attire that was dripping wet, and Jason's black leather shoes made a squishing sound with every step, while Corey walked with jerky up-and-down movements, a high-heeled sandal on one foot, the other bare.

Corey knew that those watching them were speculating on how they had got in their present condition. She would have found the tableau highly amusing had she not been so furious with Jason for his high-handed manner in handling the evening's fiasco.

They rode the elevator upward in silence, trying to ignore each other *and* the stares of two little old ladies with wide eyes and open mouths. On a sudden whimsical impulse, Corey began speaking, looking at first one and then the other with innocent eyes.

"Would you believe that we were in this *really* expensive French restaurant, and when the waiter touched a match to the cognac on our 'Cherries Jubilee,' the flames leaped so high that the next thing we knew, the automatic sprinkler system was activated and everyone was drenched! The fire alarm went off, people were yelling, waiters were running everywhere. It was awful, just awful!" Dramatically she threw her head up and back, covered her eyes with the back of one hand and shivered.

"Oh, how terrible for you, dearie!" one lady gushed, her hand fluttering near her heart. "Sara, can you imagine?"

The elevator stopped at her floor, the doors slid smoothly open, and Corey limped from the car, followed by a stony-faced Jason, then turned to give the sympathetic women a dazzling smile.

When the doors slid closed and the car had once more moved upward, Corey released the laughter that had been threatening to burst forth. She whirled around, lost her balance and was braced by Jason's strong arms as he reached out to steady her.

He led her to the door of her apartment, and Corey leaned weakly against the wall of the corridor, the delayed effects of the champagne and the events of the evening beginning to hit her. Although she wasn't drunk, everything seemed both absurd and wildly amusing. She stared uncomprehendingly at Jason as he held out his open hand, palm upward.

"Your key!" he demanded gruffly.

"Key?" Corey repeated vaguely, then collapsed into hysterical laughter. When the spasm passed, she looked at him very solemnly and shook her head from side to side. "I don't have a key," she announced mournfully.

"What do you mean you don't have a key, Corey? You live here, for God's sake!" he said, thoroughly irritated.

"I do?" she asked wonderingly. Then, looking around her, she focused her eyes on the door and read the number aloud. "Four-o-three. Oh, yeah. I suppose I do," she repeated.

"Where is your key?" Jason asked, holding on to his patience by sheer willpower.

"My key is in my purse," she intoned. "My purse is at the Venetia's. In the living room. On a table. By the vase. With pretty flowers."

Jason swore loudly, running his fingers through his hair distractedly.

"You could always take me home with you," Corey suggested, snuggling up to him. Her words were followed by a loud hiccup.

Jason tried to ignore the suggestion that had set up a clamoring within him. A part of his mind was saying "Why not? It *was* her idea." The other part was trying to remain sensible, reminding him that in her present condition it would be taking advantage of her. Under other, more sober circumstances, she would never have made such a suggestion, and he knew that if he followed through on it she would forever despise him.

Setting her firmly aside, Jason ordered Corey to stay put and headed for the elevator.

When he reached the lobby desk, he immediately recognized Miss Darcy—as Corey had called her earlier—to be the young woman who had been on duty that day, weeks ago, when he had stormed in and demanded a key to Miss Kelton's apartment.

Now, at the same request, the speed with which the woman produced a passkey and thrust it into his outstretched hand let Jason know that she had also recognized him. He nodded his thanks and turned away. At the elevator he glanced back and saw the woman staring at his wet evening clothes. She shook her head slowly, and from the look on her face Jason knew that she surely must think him perverted or demented, maybe even both.

Returning to the fourth floor, Jason stepped off the elevator and saw Corey sitting on the floor, her back against the wall, her knees drawn up and encircled by her arms, her chin resting on her knees. She smiled sweetly.

"I stayed put, just like you told me to, Jason," she chirped proudly and stood awkwardly to her feet. "You know, Jason, I used to hate it when you got bossy. But not anymore. No sirree! I'm a changed woman, and I owe it all to you," she rambled on.

Jason had now unlocked the door, and he pushed it wide open. Wordlessly he stepped aside and motioned for Corey to enter.

"Now I've decided I like you, Jason," she proclaimed. Stopping in the doorway, she looked over her shoulder at him.

Jason pushed her gently forward, urging her through the door, and followed her in. Immediately he shrugged out of his damp coat and draped it over the back of a chair. Then he jerked savagely at the bow tie that seemed to be choking him and threw it on top of the coat. His scarlet cummerbund joined the other articles of clothing.

Through it all he heard the sound of Corey's voice as she continued her monologue but didn't listen to the words. His mind was still on Sinclair and the extent of his involvement with Corey.

With an effort Jason forced himself to listen to her words, thinking that perhaps she would say something that would enlighten him.

"Oh, I know you probably don't believe that, but it's true," Corey was saying.

Limping about, she stopped suddenly and gave a vigorous kick, sending her one sandal flying through the air to land in a far corner. Then moving to the middle of the room, she dragged the heavy wet skirt upward, well above her knees, and reached up still farther under the dress and began tugging at her panty hose. But she never stopped talking.

"Yes, it is. It really— Have you ever tried to pull off a pair of wet panty hose? If you haven't don't!" she warned him seriously, momentarily withdrawing one hand from under her dress to wag her forefinger at him. "They're the very dickens—" She went on and on, grimacing as she tugged and pulled. Finally she was successful in lowering the hose to just above her knees and plopped down on a chair opposite him to drag a stocking down one leg and over her foot, then repeat the process with the other.

And there was never a break in her words.

"Another thing, Jason, you remember the time—"

"Corey?" he broke in.

"Yes, Jason?"

"You're babbling. You've had too much to drink, and you're giving me a headache."

"Well, I'm glad!" she declared with satisfaction. "Because *you*, Jason Banning, have given me a headache from the first day I laid eyes on you. Not to mention heartache."

At her words, Jason stared at her in disbelief, his own heart doing a kind of flip-flop, his throat tightening. Had he heard her correctly? And did she mean . . .

He was spellbound as Corey stood from the chair and walked with measured tread toward him, her tawny eyes holding his. She reached up her arms, encircling his neck, and molded her soft body against his.

Jason's pulse careened wildly, and desire surged within him. He could feel the soft swells of her breast, her nipples taut as they pressed against the cool wet fabric of her gown.

"Jason," Corey breathed, running her warms hands along her neck to his shoulders.

He shuddered at the maddening sensations she was evoking in him. His senses reeled at the feel of her as she rubbed herself against him. Breathy little sounds issued from her lips.

With tremendous effort Jason called on all his inner resources to help him rein his passion, to maintain control of his emotions.

"Corey, you've had too much to drink," he told her gently, firmly removing her clinging arms from his neck and setting her slightly away from him.

"No, Jason, I've had just enough," she corrected him, moving closer. She ran her hands over his chest and began working at the buttons of his shirt.

"Corey! No!" he told her sternly, stilling her busy hands by clasping them in his own.

She raised her gaze to his, and their eyes met and locked. Her tawny eyes were bright with a golden fire, her lovely face was flushed, and her lips were slightly parted. She made no attempt to hide the passion that sparkled in her eyes.

Jason's heart slammed hard against his chest. Didn't she know what she was doing to him? Of course she did! She seemed to be well practiced in the art of seduction, and he wondered just where she had learned her wiles. Sinclair? The thought stabbed savagely at him.

"Don't you want me, Jason?" she asked innocently, smiling up at him.

"Corey, honey, you don't know what you're saying," he told her through clenched teeth. He swallowed hard and cleared his throat. One more time he made a valiant attempt at self-control, which was no easy task with her lower body pressed against his in a most provocative manner.

It was fast becoming difficult for him to breathe, to prevent his own body from answering hers. One of them must keep cool, he warned himself, one of them must keep a tight rein on desire. And it would have to be him, he decided, realizing that Corey had long since lost control.

"Don't be afraid, Jason," she coaxed huskily, raising herself on tiptoe to place a kiss on his chin. "I won't bite," she murmured. "I'll only nibble." And she nipped playfully at his chin.

Jason groaned. He was fast losing his own control. So much for his words of admonishment to himself, he thought, loosening his hold on Corey's hands.

Immediately she moved his hands to her breast, pressing them to her.

"Touch me, Jason," she whispered against his lips.

And he needed no further persuasion!

He kissed her deeply, hungrily. Her tongue met his, and their desires were unleashed to run rampant.

"Oh, Corey!" he rasped against her neck, and an agonizing groan came from deep within him. His arms tightened about her, and she clung to him desperately. Dear heavens, but she felt good in his arms, her body melting against his as she yielded and surrendered to the passion that was burning out of control.

Corey was aflame. Her heart tripped against her breast, and she was being drawn into a white-hot vacuum of desire, of tantalizing sensations. The bittersweet ache within her cried out for fulfillment.

She tugged impatiently at the buttons of his shirt, then her frustration gave way to the urgency of her need, and she jerked at the collar, sending buttons flying. She pulled the shirttail free of his pants, drew the garment over his shoulders to free him of the encumberment and leaned forward, placing a moist kiss on each male nipple.

"Ahhh, Corey!" An animallike cry escaped Jason's lips, and he trembled. He was a goner and he knew it.

He slipped the narrow straps from her shoulders, and the gown fell to the floor at her feet. Jason looked at the beauty before him and caught his breath sharply. In one swift motion he swept her into his arms and carried her to the bedroom.

Putting her gently on the bed, he stood looking down at her perfect body. The only garment left to remove was a wisp of white lace panties. With shaking fingers he slipped the briefs over her rounded hips and down her silky thighs.

When she lay naked before him, Jason joined her on the bed. He took her in his arms, and his lips blazed a trail from her temples to her breasts. His mouth was warm and wet against her fevered flesh. His hands played over her body, his fingers teasing, awakening every nerve.

And Corey gloried in the lofty sensations that rippled through her.

"Oh, Jason . . . Jason . . ." she chanted huskily.

The sound of his name on her lips as she moaned with passion was driving him crazy! He rolled away from her and stood from the bed.

Corey sat up suddenly. "No," she cried in despair. "Jason, please don't leave me," she pleaded, tears misting her eyes. "I-I know what I'm doing. I want you, Jason. I want you to make love to me."

Jason smiled and leaned forward to cup her face between his hands. He brushed a kiss across her parted lips. "I'm not leaving you, Corey," he said softly. "I want you so badly. And knowing you want me . . . Corey, I'd never leave you," he assured her.

Corey watched wide-eyed as he stepped back and bent forward to take off his shoes and socks. Her eyes followed his every movement as he shed his pants and undershorts and stood naked and breathtakingly masculine before her.

"Jason, you're beautiful!" she breathed in awe.

"Beautiful?" he said with a chuckle, but the laughter died on his lips as his emerald gaze met her tawny one. "How I want you." His voice was husky with emotion. "I ache for you."

Wordlessly Corey held out her arms to him.

Their heated flesh molded together, and passion welled up within Jason as his need for the woman in his arms consumed him. He touched, kissed, teased, tasted and caressed every inch of her silken body, and she followed his lead, rewarding him with the fierce pleasure of her bittersweet torture.

Jason moved over her, his rock-hard body covering the softness of her own. Gently urging her legs apart, he positioned himself between her thighs and moved against her, his throbbing heat seeking her warm womanhood. Whispering her name, he took her with one smooth thrust.

Corey cried out, her fingers digging into his shoulders, her eyes wide with surprise. But she was not as shocked as Jason was. He stiffened and hovered over her, and Corey was terrified that he would leave her. She wrapped her legs tightly around his and pulled him back to her.

She took his mouth in a deep kiss and moved beneath him until she felt him relax and follow her rhythm. And then he was moving deep within her. She arched against him, meeting his urgent thrust. He was rapidly taking her to that lofty, faraway plane where all the secrets of passion, pleasure and fulfillment awaited.

Fantasy and reality merged, and Corey rode the crest of the waves of sensuality to surrender to ecstasy. And when she called out his name, it coincided with his calling out of her own. His body jerked and seemed to hover somewhere on that faraway plateau for a timeless moment before he shuddered uncontrollably, then collapsed against her to gather her close to his heart and kiss her damp brow.

They lay in the afterglow of lovemaking, their bodies entwined, their breathing slowly returning to normal.

"Why didn't you tell me I would be the first?" were Jason's first words, his hand stroking her shoulder lazily.

"You never asked" was her quiet reply. Then, hesitantly she asked, "Are you sorry we made love, Jason? Were you sorry to learn that I was—"

"I'm not sorry for anything," he assured her, placing a finger to her lips to still any further questions. "You gave me something unbelievably special, and I wouldn't change that for anything in the world!"

Jason ran a finger along her neck and downward, slowly circling each breast, and chuckled huskily when the rosy buds hardened at his touch. "You have no idea what having your body respond to mine does to me!"

Corey rolled on top of him, taking him by surprise. She leaned over him, closing her lips about his nipple, her teeth nipping gently.

Jason sucked in his breath sharply, and his hands tightened about her hips.

"Ahhh . . . Corey . . . you little witch!" he rasped chokingly.

"And *you* have no idea how it makes *me* feel to have you respond to me," she whispered against his lips. Jason took her mouth with an urgent kiss, and passion flamed anew.

Thirteen

Opening her eyes to the faint glow of sunlight, Corey stretched lazily and rolled over, snuggling closer to the warm body lying beside her. She studied the face of the man she loved, taking in every detail, every line. She wondered how he had acquired the small scar below his lip and reached out to touch the thread-like mark, running a finger along the line.

Jason smiled and caught her hand in his, his eyes still closed.

"Nothing romantic or adventurous," he told her in a sleepy voice, and Corey was aware that he knew her thoughts. "I fell off a horse during filming. The horse reared, I fell, and his hoof grazed me."

He opened his eyes and, bringing her hand to his lips, kissed the tip of each pink finger. "Good morning, beautiful," he told her belatedly.

Corey leaned forward and kissed the tip of his nose, each eyelid, and then brushed his lips softly. "And a good morning to you," she returned. Again she laid her lips against his, and this time it was a real kiss.

They were interrupted by the shrill ringing of the telephone, and without hesitation Jason reached for the instrument, lifted the receiver from its cradle and began speaking rapidly. "Hello, this is Miss Kelton's residence. I'm sorry, but she is unable to come to the phone at this time... Er, she's otherwise engaged. But if you'll leave your name, telephone number and— Oh, hello, Cappy," Jason greeted the caller and smiled at Corey, who was still flushed from their kiss.

She snatched the receiver from his hand and sang out, "Hello, Cappy. What? Oh yes, I'm fine...." But her real attention was riveted on Jason, and she stared hard when he rose from the bed and stretched his lithe body. His nude beauty sent a shiver of anticipation cascading down her spine. "Huh? Yes, Cappy, I'm here...."

It was extremely difficult to follow the conversation, under the existing circumstances, and when Jason leaned over and kissed her breast, Corey caught her breath sharply.

"No, no, everything's fine. I will, Cappy...."

Jason disappeared into the bathroom, and within minutes Corey heard the shower and Jason's loud, boisterous voice singing, of all things, "Ninety-nine Bottles of Beer."

"After last night, I have hopes. I'm going to tell him—" The chime of the doorbell sounded, bringing her words to a halt. "Someone's at the door, Cappy. I have to go."

Again the musical tone resounded, and Corey hung up the phone and hurriedly grabbed a robe. Slipping into it quickly, she belted it about her slim waist as she ran to answer the door.

As was her habit, she placed one eye to the peephole to identify her caller. The glistening black hair and handsome face belonged to Stefan. Knowing her usually cautious nature, he knew that she would peep first, and he stood there with a wide grin, smiling straight at the blank wooden barrier he faced.

A delighted smile lit Corey's lovely face, and she flung the door wide in welcome to her friend.

He stood leaning casually against the doorframe, a mischievous smile lurking at the corners of his mouth. One hand rested in his pants pocket while from the other dangled her wayward sandal, swinging from his finger by the ankle strap.

"I'm Prince Charming, ma'am," Stefan drawled, bowing exaggeratedly, "and I'm looking for Cinderella."

Corey laughed spontaneously, ushered him in and closed the door behind them.

"And how's my favorite lady and drinking buddy this fine morning?" Stefan asked, giving her cheek a peck.

He settled himself on the sofa, and his black eyes swept over the room and came to rest on Jason's discarded clothing.

"I take it Jason stayed the night?"

"Yes," Corey breathed the one-word answer, but her dazzling smile and the vigorous nod of her head spoke volumes.

Her shining face and sparkling eyes told him what he wanted to know, but he knew Corey would expect him to ask, anyway. So he did. "So how did it all turn out?"

"Wonderful!" she replied quickly. "Just wonderful!" Her words were punctuated with a couple of whirls as she spun about on her bare toes.

"Ah-ha! I thought so! Well, you have me to thank for that, you know." With his spontaneous grin, he began to tick off the reasons on his fingers as he enumerated them. "Number one, I went out of my way to make an enemy of a guy I could really like. Two, I ruined a perfectly good tuxedo—they are not machine washable, you know. Three, I took a chance of catching my death of cold by cavorting in a cold pool. And four, which, by the way, was a double whammy, I got socked in the jaw and knocked into the water for the second time! Oh, and last but not least, I'm in heap big trouble with Uncle Mario for spoiling his party. My own flesh and blood wants me to 'take a long walk on a short pier.' His words, not mine. So I ask you, Cork, was all my suffering worth the result?''

Corey's lilting laughter reached Jason's ears as he stepped from the shower. Quickly he toweled himself dry, slipped into his rumpled pants and moved toward the living room, naked from the waist up except for the hand towel draped about his neck.

"All your, ah, suffering was indeed worth it, Stefan. And you're absolutely right. I *do* owe it all to you! If you hadn't made him so insanely jealous, Jason might not have admitted his interest in me. Thank you for helping me make my dream come true."

As she spoke, Corey walked to the sofa and sat down beside Stefan, impulsively throwing both arms around his neck. He returned her sisterly embrace, and it was at that moment Jason opened the bedroom door.

The scene before him caused him to stop dead in his tracks and anger burned within him, robbing him of rational thought. His anger-hazed mind misinterpreted it to be a lover's embrace, and he spat out a low, vehement oath.

The sound had an immediate effect. Both Corey and Stefan swung around to stare in dismay at the obviously irate man in the doorway who looked an awful lot like an enraged bull readying to charge.

"Jason!" Corey sprang from the sofa and hastened toward him. "Stefan came by to return my shoe and to see if, ah, to see if I was all right," she explained in a rush.

Jason's heated gaze ran over her, taking in the thin robe that clung to her softly rounded curves and his anger soared when he realized she wore nothing beneath it.

"I think you'd better get dressed," he advised, his voice low and threatening. He moved from the doorway, allowing her entrance to her bedroom.

"Jason—"

"*Now*, Corey!" he bit out the order.

Corey cast a quick glance at Stefan before leaving the room.

In the bedroom she hurriedly pulled a shirt and jeans from the closet while warily watching Jason, who hadn't moved from the doorway.

He stood with his back to her but not a word did he speak to Stefan, whom he was facing. His back was rigid, ramrod straight, and there was resentment in every line of his taut body.

There was complete silence as Jason held Stefan's open gaze for an endless time, then walked back into the bedroom. Still without a word, not even looking in Corey's direction, he retrieved his shoes and socks from the floor and dropped the towel from around his neck. In the living room he gathered up the remainder of his clothes and walked out the door.

Barefoot, bare-chested, his odd assortment of clothing held loosely in one hand and shoes and socks in the other, Jason stepped from the elevator at the ground-floor level. He strode across the lobby to the desk where, once again, he was face-to-face with a wide-eyed, openmouthed, white-faced Miss Darcy.

"I need to use the phone," he said matter-of-factly. But the woman didn't budge, just stood staring at him as if he were something straight from the *Twilight Zone*. "The phone, Miss Darcy."

The woman shook visibly as she picked up the telephone and placed it on the counter. She backed away, her large eyes darting about the room, as if seeking help.

After calling his chauffeur, Jason walked across the lobby and settled down on the oversize sofa where he proceeded to dress himself, indifferent to his surroundings, uncaring of his audience. When he pulled on his shirt, his fingers automatically reached for the nonexistent buttons. This brought to his memory Corey's eager hands on him, her whimpers as she tried to work the buttons loose and her impatience when she had literally ripped the shirt open, sending the buttons flying.

On the heels of that memory came another. Their night of passion when they had made love over and over throughout the long night. Physically exhausted, they had fallen asleep in the wee hours of the morning, entwined in a lovers' embrace. Then had come the sweetness of waking up with Corey at his side—

And then he had walked in and found her in Sinclair's arms!

"Jason."

Stefan's low voice snapped him from his wonderings, and Jason stared up at the man, unveiled dislike firing his green eyes.

His own gaze never wavering from the heat of the killing glare, Stefan seated himself in the chair opposite Jason and leaned forward to speak to him without being overheard.

"Jason, I'd like—"

"I have nothing to say to you, Sinclair, and I have no desire to hear whatever you have to say to me," Jason broke in curtly.

"What I have to say to you, you need to hear, my friend," Stefan spoke firmly, choosing not to be intimidated.

"I'm *not* your friend, Sinclair," Jason gritted.

"Then allow me to be yours," the other man returned calmly. "There's a beautiful woman crying upstairs because her heart is breaking. You may not give a damn, but I do! I love Corey Kelton," he said bluntly.

As he knew it would, Stefan's last statement gained Jason's full attention and, once he had it, he hurried on. "I've loved her for a good many years. I've held her with compassion while she cried, held her hand with reassurance when she wasn't confident enough to go it alone. The strength of our friendship has comforted us both during times of loneliness. In short, my love for Corey is that of a brother.

"And, Jason Banning, I'm not going to stand by and see her made unhappy! She means too much to me to allow you to hurt her. You grossly misconstrued what you saw earlier. And in your unwarranted jealousy and insecurity where Corey is concerned, you were blind to the truth. You were unfair to walk out without allowing either of us the benefit of explanation!"

Corey lay facedown across her bed, her pillow wet with tears. How could things have gone so terribly wrong, she wondered. She had soared joyously to the heavens and plummeted to heretofore unknown depths in a very short span of time. And all because Jason Banning would not trust, and refused to listen to truth and reason.

But now there were no more tears, and they hadn't helped, anyway. Her heart was still sore, and she was still alone. She had hoped that Jason would have second thoughts and at least let her explain.

She rolled over and sat up, surveying the unmade bed. She reached out and ran her hand over the extra pillow where Jason's head had rested. Her gaze moved on to rest on the wispy white lace panties that had been hastily disposed of last night. Everything reminded her of Jason.

With an effort Corey stood from the bed and was suddenly overtaken with a strange giddiness and quickly sat down. She knew that it was caused by too much crying and no food. Glancing at the bedside clock, she saw that the time was a bit past noon.

At the sound of the doorbell, she was filled with renewed hope that the caller would be Jason. Once more the chimes rang out, and she hurried to the door. She pressed her eye to the peephole which revealed Stefan, grinning widely and looking straight at the tiny opening.

Corey turned the lock and opened the door to see that Stefan was laden with large brown grocery bags.

"Hi, gorgeous," Stefan greeted her, pausing only to hastily brush her cheek with his own before heading for the small kitchen, with Corey following close on his heels.

"If I know Cork, she hasn't eaten today. And she dearly *loves* Chinese food. So I went to this restaurant that has take-out food and got a little bit of everything they had."

As he talked, Stefan busily removed carton after carton of pleasant-smelling food and set them out on the bar. Turning to the stove, he grabbed the teakettle, filled it with water and set it to boil. He pulled out a couple of cabinet drawers before he located the silver, then opened an overhead door to find cups for their tea. And he carried on a one-sided conversation all the while.

Perched on a bar stool, Corey watched more eagerly than she had thought possible. She had thought she had no appetite but soon learned she was wrong. She followed Stefan's efficient movements, and by the time they were ready to eat, she was ravenous.

Stefan's running monologue covered a variety of subjects, and he moved from one to the other so smoothly that soon Corey was drawn into the conversation almost without being aware of it.

Before long they were talking easily, and Corey's spirits were lifted. Things didn't look so bleak anymore. There was no doubt about it, Corey thought, Stefan was good for her and she remembered that he'd always been able to make her laugh.

"Well, milady, shall we retire to the parlor to finish our tea?" Stefan asked. Placing a tea towel over his arm with a flourish, he picked up the teapot in one hand and his cup in the other, preceding her as they left the kitchen.

Stefan had no intention of allowing Corey to dwell on the events of the previous night and the morning hours just past. He was there to occupy her time and distract her thoughts. He had done what he could to set Jason straight, and if the man had any sense, and Stefan knew that he did, he'd see things as they really were. It might take awhile, but Stefan was betting on Jason.

Loyal friend that he was, Stefan didn't leave Corey alone. He stayed throughout the afternoon and kept her thoughts off the movie, off her problems—off Jason.

Only once did Corey broach the subject of Jason, and the thought and fresh memories caused her to break into tears. Stefan comforted her, not by sympathizing, but by assuring her that the situation was only temporary and that Jason would soon come to his senses. She dried her tears and promised to trust Stefan's judgement.

And not until the sun was low in the west and he had seen Corey stifle a few yawns did Stefan take his leave.

"It's been a long day, and yours truly is tired," he told her, yawning openly for her benefit. "Why don't you take a shower and go to bed," Stefan advised softly. "I'll tidy up and let myself out."

"Thank you, Stefan," Corey whispered, "for everything!"

Placing a tender kiss upon his cheek, she sleepily made her way to the bedroom.

Fourteen

Jason's confrontation with Sinclair in the lobby of Corey's building had certainly given him new insight. Stefan hadn't been intimidated by him and had more or less forced Jason to hear him out. Another situation where Jason Banning hadn't been in control, he thought wryly. Stefan had accused Jason of being unfair, something Jason Banning had never been branded before. Actually, he had always prided himself on his fairness.

At the same time that accusation had been made, his chauffeur had arrived, and Jason had impulsively asked Stefan if he could drop him someplace. Sinclair had hit a nerve, and Jason wanted to exonerate himself.

On the drive to Mario Venetia's, each man had opportunity to plumb the depths of the other, and by the time they reached their destination, each had gained the genuine respect of the other.

Jason's pride hadn't allowed him to return to Corey's apartment, and he knew that it might have been a mistake. But he simply hadn't felt himself ready to deal with his emotions or hers. He'd gone back to the studio and retrieved the metal box from his safe and locked it in the trunk of his car.

Later, he had shown up on Edith's doorstep, looking as if he'd lost his last friend. Over coffee and sandwiches with John and Edith, he filled them in on everything that had happened since they'd seen him leave the Venetia estate with Corey.

Jason had surprised them with the startling information that he liked Sinclair. He'd explained the real relationship between Stefan and Corey, and in the telling, he recognized that the other man had helped Corey through some very trying times when she had had no one. Jason had realized that he truly appreciated the kind of friend Stefan was, and had been, to the woman Jason loved.

Upon leaving the Ward residence, Jason had returned to his own home to pace the floor. In his mind's eye he could see the stricken look on Corey's face when he ordered her to her room to get dressed. How could he have been so dense? he asked himself. He *had* been unfair, as Sinclair had stated. Hadn't he learned only a few hours before that Corey was untouched? She'd known Stefan a long time and obviously loved him a great deal. So? So if sex had been a part of her feelings for Stefan Sinclair, Jason Banning wouldn't have been the first last night. It was that simple.

He owed Corey an apology and during the afternoon had picked up the telephone a dozen or more times to call her. Each time he replaced the receiver, afraid that she wouldn't talk to him. He couldn't take her rejection, even though he knew he probably deserved it.

Jason had refused to answer his own telephone, even though it had rung persistently. Finally he had turned off the bell, putting an end to the shrill summons. He didn't want to talk to anyone about anything until he had straightened things out with Corey, and he needed time to think everything through.

The long afternoon dragged on interminably. From the corner of the sofa where he slouched, Jason picked up the remote control for the television and turned it on. After watching the show briefly, he began pushing the buttons on the control from channel to channel. Program after program flickered across the wide screen, but nothing held his attention for long. With a groan of exasperation he turned the set off and tossed the control aside.

In the kitchen, he plucked an apple from a bowl of fruit on the bar and spied a plate piled high with brownies. It was his housekeeper's day off, and Jason smiled at her obvious concern for him.

He meandered back into the living room and picked up the screenplay that had been delivered earlier. It was *Rainbow Rider*, Mario Venetia's pet project. He wanted Jason for the male lead and was considering Corey for the female lead. "There's a volatile chemistry between you two," Venetia had declared loudly, slapping Jason on the back. "That chemistry will come across on the screen, and the audience will love it. It's all there, the combination of heated intimacy, charged tension, spontaneous temperaments and fire!"

Yes, it *was* all there, and nobody knew it better than Jason. He'd shared the heated intimacy, felt the tension, experienced the spontaneous temperaments and, above all, had touched and been touched by that all-consuming fire.

Jason knew that Corey was hoping to be cast as the female lead in the movie and wondered if fate would allow them to make another Banning-Kelton film. Or if fate would allow a Banning-Kelton *anything*.

He sat down to read the script but after only a few pages realized he hadn't retained anything he'd read. He threw it aside in annoyance.

Late in the evening Jason showered and stepped dripping wet from the bathroom. Not bothering with a towel, he crossed the bedroom to sprawl naked across his bed leaving a trail of water behind him. He lay flat on his back, his gaze fixed on the ceiling, his mind running rampant with memories, what ifs, and regrets.

For hours Jason tossed restlessly and sleep wouldn't come. He got up and dressed; he didn't know why, since a glance at the clock showed the time to be half-past midnight. He needed some fresh air, he needed some rest, and he needed to do something, go somewhere. He needed Corey! Knowing his mind was too cluttered with his thoughts and regrets to concentrate on driving, he called his chauffeur from a sound sleep, apologized, then asked him to bring the car around.

The sleek black limo moved smoothly through the streets. Jason had told the driver that there was no hurry and no destination. And for the better part of an hour he had simply been driven around.

The night lights, twinkling and glimmering, were reflected in the tinted windows, and dancing shadows invaded the interior of the car.

From time to time Jason rested his hand on the metal box that sat on the seat beside him. He mentally rehearsed what he had to tell Corey and wondered what her reaction would be. She would be greatly affected by the actual proof of Matt's deception.

He had procrastinated long enough, Jason decided with a sigh. More time wouldn't help, nor would it change the result of his meeting with Corey, whatever it might be. And he needed to get it behind him. At least he wouldn't have to wonder and worry about Corey's reaction, because an hour from now it could be history.

Picking up the intercom phone, Jason spoke to the chauffeur.

"Regency House."

Although relaxed and sleepy, once Corey climbed between her sheets, she became wide-awake. Her memories were too raw, too fresh. Less than twelve hours before, she had been initiated into womanhood by the man she loved most.

The soft glow of the street light dimly lit her bedroom, and the ceiling became her movie screen. Staring upward, she watched as last night's passionate love scene was replayed in her mind's eye. On the heels of that memory came the devastating scene involving dear innocent Stefan.

"Oh, Jason," Corey moaned aloud. "Why couldn't you trust me? Why wouldn't you believe me? Why did you refuse to listen to truth and reason?"

As she heard herself speak the words aloud, they suddenly hit home. Hadn't that been exactly what she'd done when Jason had tried so earnestly to explain his role in the takeover of Fielder Studios? Had she trusted him? Had she believed? And hadn't she stubbornly refused to listen to truth and reason?

She remembered how Jason's troubled eyes had beseeched her and recalled the ring of truth in his words and the patience he had exerted in trying to get through to her. In return she'd flung hateful, bitter accusations in his face and had tried his endurance to the breaking point. Remorse washed over her, and she moaned, thinking of the hopelessness of the whole wretched mess.

Despite all her efforts, Corey couldn't sleep. The bedside clock showed that it was nearly ten o'clock. She tried to think of other things; however, each glance at the clock revealed that only a few minutes had elapsed since she last looked.

The musical peal of the doorbell roused her, and Corey was surprised to find that she had actually fallen asleep. Slipping into her robe, she smiled on her way to the door. It was probably Stefan, she thought. Most likely he had been driving by and had stopped to share her misery.

Her eye to the peephole, she gasped. Were her eyes deceiving her, or had she dwelt on thoughts of Jason to the extent that she had conjured him up?

With a feeling of apprehension, she slowly opened the door to see Jason standing in the hallway, his face drawn and tired. In his hand he held a small metal case.

"May I come in, Corey?" he asked wearily.

Without a word she stepped back. She closed the door and leaned against it uncertainly for a moment, watching Jason move across the room and set the box on the coffee table.

Jamming his hands into his pockets, he turned to see that Corey hadn't moved from the door. Their eyes met in question.

"Would you like some coffee?" she ventured, not knowing why he was there.

"If it isn't too much trouble."

Grateful to be busy, Corey hurried to the kitchen to make the coffee. Her hands shook as she scooped coffee into the percolator, and when Jason walked in, she spilled brown granules on the countertop.

He noted that Corey's eyes darted to the metal box in his hand, and he set it down on the bar, pushing it toward her.

"This will be a little like opening Pandora's box. I know, because it was that way for me when I opened it," Jason told her gravely. "This is one of the reasons I'm here. This box holds information I learned only a few days ago. Since then I've been trying to find the words to tell you, a way to soften the shock that you're bound to feel."

As he sat down heavily on a bar stool, Corey drew the mysterious box nearer. Although curious, she felt the same apprehension she'd experienced earlier when she'd seen Jason in the hall.

"I went through everything there and meant to file away everything that seemed unimportant, but I wanted you to see it just as I found it."

Taking a deep breath, Corey lifted the lid and began going through the contents. Her eyes tearful, she scanned the battered snapshots, letters that she had written to Matt, glanced at the old lease agreements, but saw nothing that would be a shocking secret. She raised confused, questioning eyes to Jason.

"There's only one document in all that clutter that's truly important," Jason stated, reaching for the stack of papers she had nervously sifted through.

Knowing exactly what to look for, he soon extracted it from the jumbled mass and held it in his hand, making no move to give it to her. "Maybe I'd best lay a bit of groundwork before you look at this."

Jason began the story....

Corey sat in stunned silence. Of all the reasons that had gone through her mind about why Jason had come to her, this was nothing like what she had imagined it might be.

Silent tears slid down her cheeks. Now all the pieces had fallen in place, and the picture wasn't a pleasant one. Matt, her dear Matt whom she had loved, trusted, respected and had remained loyal to, had not only deceived her but had cheated her. Matt had abused her father's trust.

She wasn't crying for Matt or for herself, but for her dear father and for Jason, who at this very moment held in his hand proof of a secret that had remained so for all these years.

Jason could have destroyed that document, she realized, and the secret would have lived on. No one would have been the wiser. He could have taken it all, yet he had not. Jason was a person of integrity, and he wasn't capable of such deceit. He had given her what rightfully belonged to her, something that had been deliberately withheld from her.

Because of his selfless act, she loved this wonderful man even more, if that were possible.

"And that's the whole of it, Corey," Jason concluded.

He stared earnestly at her, waiting for a reaction. When there was none, no word spoken, no movement made, he became uneasy. He wanted to reach out to her, to assure her that he was there for her. It was pure hell to stand by and read the mixture of emotions playing across her face—the pain, the disbelief, the disillusion.

"So what you are saying is that I have owned half of the studio since my father died, and Matt—" Her voice broke achingly, and she bit down on her lower lip to still its quivering. "Matt deliberately cheated me all those years," she stated, drawing a deep, steadying breath. "I've blamed you, Jason, for so much and all without cause. I felt cheated; you had walked in to pull the rug out from under my dreams, and I hated you." She raised tear-bright eyes to him. "I'm sorry, Jason. Sorry for so many things."

"Corey—" Jason began, his words ceasing abruptly at the shaking of her head.

She clutched the envelope to her breast and walked out of the kitchen, through the living room and into her bedroom without a backward glance.

Jason let her go, although his heart was crying out to stop her, to take her in his arms and assure her that everything would be all right. But he knew she needed to be alone, to sort this all out for herself. This time no one would be there to protect her from reality, but he would be here waiting with open heart and outstretched arms to offer all his love.

Staring down at the cold coffee in his mug, Jason realized that more than half an hour had passed since Corey had retreated to the solitude of her bedroom, and he'd heard no sound. He stood and walked toward the bedroom.

Pausing in the open doorway, he saw Corey sitting on the bed in the shadows, the damning document lying forgotten upon her lap. Sensing his presence, she looked up, an uncertain smile on her lips, and Jason moved to sit beside her.

"I didn't know Matthew Fielder at all," she announced flatly. She folded the paper and replaced it in the envelope. "You could have kept this information from me, Jason, just as Matt did. But you chose to give me back what was my dream." Corey's gaze held his in the semidarkness. "I don't have the money to repay the part of the loan I'm responsible for, but I—"

"I don't hold you accountable for that money, Corey," Jason said quietly, taking her cold hands in the warmth of his own. "You had no knowledge of Matt's treachery and you're not indebted to me."

"Oh, but I am, Jason," she countered. "I owe you—"

"I don't want anything from you, Corey!"

"Nothing?" she asked anxiously.

"Yes! There's so much I want from you, but it's out of my reach. Money, the studio—those things have nothing to do with what I want, what I need, Corey. I came over here to give you that damned box and show you the agreement that proves your ownership of the studio. Because of my dealings with Matt Fielder, I'm your partner, but if you don't want that partnership I'll hand the whole thing to you. I'd walk away from it and never look back. It isn't the studio that's important to me."

"The studio," Corey laughed softly. "Funny how dreams fade. The studio is mine, now, and I don't even care, I don't want it anymore."

"You don't—"

"Not now that I've found something so much more important," Corey said honestly, raising her hand to touch his cheek. "I love you, Jason," she whispered, so softly that Jason wasn't quite sure he'd heard correctly. "I've loved you since I was sixteen and I ran into your car and headlong into love. I've fought that love for so long. And I don't want to fight it anymore," she said with a catch in her voice. "I want you to love me and I think you do. Please, Jason, tell me I haven't come this far only to lose what I want and need so desperately."

"No, my darling," the words were soft, caressing. "What that beautiful young woman who ran into love some eight years ago doesn't know is that she hasn't been alone in her love or in her need." He gently cupped her face within his hands, brushing her trembling lips with his thumb. "I love you, Corey," Jason breathed the words. "There hasn't been a day that I haven't loved you with all my heart."

He loved her! Jason had spoken the words with quiet conviction. The truth of his words was there, shining in his eyes, it was in his touch, in the velvety timbre of his voice.

She had loved him for so long! She had wanted, needed his love and now—Corey's eyes shimmered with tears as she reached out, her trembling fingers caressing his face.

"Oh, Jason," Corey cried. She leaned toward him and, when he closed his arms around her, melted against him. Her heart, her body, her soul surrendered unquestioningly to Jason. She did not love alone!

Jason held Corey to his strength, to his heart, and when their lips met in an urgent kiss, all else was forgotten.

"Corey...Corey..." Jason whispered against her lips, her name a ragged, breathless sound. "Ah, my sweet love, my heart, my life." The words were hushed and urgent as he trailed fiery kisses down her throat, along the satiny smoothness of her shoulder and the soft swell of her breasts.

Jason's hands, warm and arousing, moved over her with urgency, knowing just what touch would ignite the passion within her. His skilled fingers moved over her back and along her sides, his thumbs teasing the edges of her breasts. Her body cried out to him, needing his touch and an aching, reckless hunger claimed her.

Corey moved closer, her fingers groping at the buttons of Jason's shirt, a whimper tearing at her throat. She wanted to touch him, feel his heated flesh. She needed him as never before.

Jason kissed her deeply, his tongue dipping into the warm sweetness of her mouth and she hungrily met his kiss. He pulled away, his lips and tongue teasing hers as she tried to recapture his mouth, to savor the kiss and he chuckled softly at her unspoken plea.

"Do you want me, Corey?" Jason whispered against her mouth as he nibbled at her lower lip.

"Yes...ohh, yes I want you," she breathed. "I ache with it, I—" Her words were lost in the depths of his kiss.

Jason eased the straps of the teddy from her shoulders and the satiny fabric whispered over her breasts as it slipped downward, coming to rest at her trim waist. He caught his breath sharply at the sight before him.

Corey's breasts were full, their dusky crests erect with arousal as they beckoned his touch. A groan came from deep in his throat as he reached out to cup them gently, weighing their ripe softness in the palms of his hands as he stroked hardened nipples with his thumbs. Bending his dark head, he traced each swell with the tip of his tongue. He smiled knowingly as a shudder ran through Corey and she breathed his name as softly as a caress.

Jason lifted his head, yet his hands didn't still their sensual play. He held her passion-filled gaze with the emerald fire of his own eyes. "How I want you!" His words were choked, his breath ragged and shallow. "I'm going to make love to you, Corey. Long, sweet, and slow.'' His eyes continued to hold hers, passion smoldering in their depths. "I'm going to make love to you the way I have so many times in my dreams, in my fantasies."

As he spoke, Jason drew the teddy over her flat stomach and along her shapely legs, tossing it to the floor. "I have years of need in me, Corey," he said huskily as he stood from the bed and slowly began stripping his clothes. "I'm going to make up for all the desire, all the passion, all the yearning. I want to taste all that I've missed, all that I've longed for for so many years."

Corey watched, mesmerized by his deliberate, seductive movements. Her blood ran hotly through her veins, her heart raced in her breast. And when Jason stood naked and unashamed before her, Corey caught her breath at the sheer male beauty of him and the evidence of his arousal. Her gaze ran over him, desire flared in her brown eyes. Wordlessly she opened her arms to him.

Jason's heated flesh seared hers as he pressed her to the softness of the bed, his hands blazed a trail of fire over her silken flesh. He brushed warm kisses along the path his hands had taken, his lips caressing her, exciting her, awakening her body to sensuality, to ecstasy. Corey was on fire, the need for him consuming her as he stroked, teased and aroused her to the brink of madness.

An exquisite tension was building within him as he explored the silken softness of her pliant body. Jason fought for control, reining the driving desire mounting within him. Never had he felt such passion, such need. This was his woman, his love, his life. After all the years, the loneliness of loving alone, never touching, never tasting the love—the feel of her in his arms, the taste of her was beyond belief! It was right, so very right. It had always been Corey. There had never been another. Never had he given a woman his love, never had he made *love*.

"You've always been mine, Corey," Jason rasped passionately. "How I want you, how I love you!"

Corey writhed beneath him, her movements luring him on, her fingers digging into his back as she pressed closer and closer to his heat. Her teeth nipped at his throat and shoulders. "Please," she panted breathlessly. "Please, Jason."

"Slowly, my love. Slowly," Jason whispered huskily.

Grasping both her hands, he held them over her head and with one of his. He smiled and with maddening slowness he ran his other hand lightly over her breasts, along her taut belly and stroked her inner thighs.

"Long, sweet, slow..." he reminded her. Jason felt her shudder uncontrollably, causing a current to rip through him and he watched as Corey bit her lower lip and moaned deeply. When his searching fingers found the warmth of her woman's core, her breath quickened and she arched wildly against his hand, calling his name.

"Ah, Corey, what you do to me," he rasped and with a ragged groan hungrily kissed her parted lips. Jason covered her with his body, her supple softness molding to the hard contours of his muscular frame. Corey wriggled, squirmed and rubbed against him in an age-old rhythm of woman's need of man, igniting a painfully sweet fire within him.

There was no holding back as Jason's desire rushed forth with overwhelming intensity, sweeping over him with such force that it took his breath away. His blood raced, his heart pounded. He had to have her, he could wait no longer.

Jason surged forward, filling Corey with his hardness, imbedding himself in the center of her feminine heat and slowly, deliberately moved within her.

Lifting her hips from the bed, Corey arched her back as she met Jason's thrusts, causing a rapture of flames to lick through Jason and the desire she evoked in him was staggering. He moaned with pleasure and clenched his teeth, willing himself to prolong their passion.

Again and again, Corey arched against him, meeting him, desire mounting to a fevered pitch as she became enmeshed with him in a passion that could not, would not, be denied. Her hands roamed his body, her fingers trailed along his spine, across his buttocks and over his sides as she stroked and kneaded his flesh.

She kissed his chest, his shoulders, his neck, exploring every part of him with her hands, lips and tongue. She felt a throbbing within her, a raw, almost savage hunger that cried out for release. And when Jason's strokes became firmer, deeper, and he clasped her to him, his thrusts quickening, Corey's body was responsive. He took her higher and higher, to the lofty plains of complete rapture.

Jason's breath stilled, only to rush forth in a gasp. A heat centered within and welled upward, pulsating through him as spasms of pleasure shot through his body and he came to a thundering release just as Corey reached hers.

Corey clung to him and felt the stiffening of his body as he seemed to hang suspended above her. She had given all, held back nothing and she realized that Jason had done the same.

Jason rolled from her and cradled Corey within his arms. He kissed her moist brow and tightened the embrace as a tremor stole over her. He had loved her with abandonment. With his heart, body and soul he had given as much as he took. He had surrendered himself completely to the ecstasy of their lovemaking. Two people could never be as close as he and Corey were in that moment. How he loved her!

As the silvery fingers of dawn streaked across the morning sky, Jason stirred and moved from Corey's embrace, chuckling at her whimper of protest as he eased himself off the bed. He stood and stretched, the muscles rippling beneath his tanned flesh. Combing his fingers through his tousled hair, he yawned widely and crossed the room to bend over and get his pants from the floor. He retrieved a small package from the pocket and returned to the bed.

Jason stood looking long and lovingly at the sleeping woman and love swelled within him, threatening to steal his breath. He leaned over and placed tiny kisses on her neck and shoulder. When she rolled onto her back, sighing and stretching lazily, Jason captured an upthrust breast in his hand and kissed the rosy crest.

Wrapping her arms about him, Corey pulled him closer as she whispered his name sleepily.

"Hmm?"

"Jason, am I dreaming?"

"Open your eyes, my love, and you'll see I'm still here," he suggested.

Corey stared deep into his emerald eyes, which shone with such tender love that she caught her breath.

"Hi!"

"Hi, yourself," Corey returned and kissed him loudly.

"Corey?"

"Yes, Jason."

"You will? Hallelujah!" he shouted and rained kisses on her face.

"Hallelujah? I will what?"

"Marry me!" he stated, a wide smile on his face. "You said you'd marry me."

"I did no such thing!" Corey countered with surprise.

"You did so. You said 'Yes, Jason.' I heard you."

"Jason, I—"

"Why won't you marry me, Corey?"

"You didn't ask."

"Oh, all right. I, Jason Richard Banning, being of sound mind—"

"That's doubtful," she interjected and looked all round-eyed and innocent when Jason scowled at her.

"Like I said, being of sound mind and hopelessly in love with the beautiful and very naked woman beside me, hereby ask, at her request, the following. Corey, will you marry me?"

"What woman being of sound mind could refuse? Yes, Jason, I will marry you." And she sealed her words with a kiss.

She stared down at something Jason laid upon her breast. "What—"

"It isn't an engagement ring, honey. We'll go shopping for that this afternoon. There was one other item in the box," Jason said quietly. "It was something very special. Go ahead, open it," he encouraged.

Corey opened the package, not knowing what to expect, and when the wrapping was removed to unveil its hidden treasure, she cried out. There, nestled on a cloud of cotton, lay a gold-and-diamond heart-shaped locket. Tears misted her eyes when she read, "Sweet Sixteen," and overflowed when she turned the locket over and read the inscription.

Wordlessly she handed the locket to Jason, and he understood her unspoken request. He clasped the slender gold chain around her neck, his warm hands resting on her shoulders.

Raising tear-misted eyes to him, she whispered, "Jason."

Any further words she might have spoken were stopped by Jason's lips against hers in a tender kiss, and she surrendered her heart, body and soul to Jason's touch.

*　*　*　*　*

Silhouette Desire

**Available
August 1987**

ONE TOUGH HOMBRE

Visit with characters introduced
in the acclaimed Desire trilogy
by Joan Hohl!

The *Hombre* is back!
J. B. Barnet—first introduced in *Texas Gold*—
has returned and make no mistake,
J.B. is one tough hombre . . . but
Nicole Vanzant finds the gentle,
tender side of the former
Texas Ranger.

Don't miss *One Tough Hombre*—
J.B. and Nicole's story.
And coming soon from Desire is
Falcon's Flight—the story of Flint Falcon
and Leslie Fairfield.

D372-1R

Silhouette Desire

COMING NEXT MONTH

#373 INTRUSIVE MAN—Lass Small
How could Hannah Calhoun continue to run her boardinghouse with any semblance of sanity when all her paying guests were pushing her into the all-too-willing arms of Officer Maxwell Simmons?

#374 HEART'S DELIGHT—Ashley Summers
Cabe McLain was resigned to a life of single parenthood—but that was before Laura Richards showed him that her childhood friendship had ripened into a woman's love.

#375 A GIFT OF LOVE—Sherryl Woods
Meg Blake had learned early on that most problems were best dealt with alone. Matt Flanagan was the one to show her otherwise—teaching her firsthand the power of love.

#376 SOMETHING IN COMMON—Leslie Davis Guccione
Confirmed bachelor Kevin Branigan, the "cranberry baron" from STILL WATERS (Desire #353), met Erin O'Connor—and more than met his match!

#377 MEET ME AT MIDNIGHT—Christine Flynn
Security agent Matt Killian did things by-the-book. He had no intention of having an unpredictable—and all too attractive—Eden Michaels on his team. But soon Matt found himself throwing caution to the winds.

#378 THE PRIMROSE PATH—Joyce Thies
It took an outrageous scheme from their respective grandparents to find the adventurous hearts beneath banker Clay Chancelor's and CPA Carla Valentine's staid exteriors. Neither imagined that the prize at the end of the chase was love.

AVAILABLE NOW:

#367 ADAM'S STORY
Annette Broadrick

#368 ANY PIRATE IN A STORM
Suzanne Carey

#369 FOREVER MINE
Selwyn Marie Young

#370 PARTNERS FOR LIFE
Helen R. Myers

#371 JASON'S TOUCH
Sheryl Flournoy

#372 ONE TOUGH HOMBRE
Joan Hohl

ATTRACTIVE, SPACE SAVING BOOK RACK

Display your most prized novels on this handsome and sturdy book rack. The hand-rubbed walnut finish will blend into your library decor with quiet elegance, providing a practical organizer for your favorite hard-or soft-covered books.

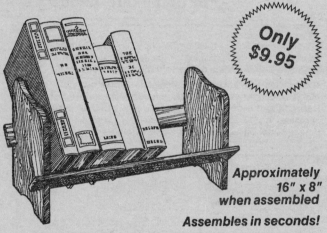

Only $9.95

Approximately 16" x 8" when assembled

Assembles in seconds!

To order, rush your name, address and zip code, along with a check or money order for $10.70* ($9.95 plus 75¢ postage and handling) payable to *Silhouette Books*.

Silhouette Books
Book Rack Offer
901 Fuhrmann Blvd.
P.O. Box 1396
Buffalo, NY 14269-1396

BKR-2A

Offer not available in Canada.

*New York and Iowa residents add appropriate sales tax.

Desire™ PROOF-OF-PURCHASE

FREE!
Never Before Published

Silhouette Desire™
by Stephanie James!

A year ago she left for the city. Now he's come to claim her back. Read about it in SAXON'S LADY, available exclusively through this offer. This book will not be sold through retail stores.

To participate in this exciting offer, collect three proof-of-purchase coupons from the back pages of July and August Desire titles. Mail in the three coupons plus $1.00 for postage and handling ($1.25 in Canada) to reserve your copy of this unique book. This special offer expires October 31, 1987.

Mail to: Silhouette Reader Service

In the U.S.A.
901 Fuhrmann Blvd.
P.O. Box 1397
Buffalo, N.Y. 14240

In Canada
P.O. Box 609
Fort Erie, Ontario
L2A 9Z9

Please send me my special copy of SAXON'S LADY. I have enclosed the three Desire coupons required and $1.00 for postage and handling ($1.25 in Canada) along with this order form. (Please Print)

NAME _____

ADDRESS _____

CITY _____

STATE/PROV. _____ ZIP/POSTAL CODE _____

SIGNATURE _____

This offer is limited to one order per household.   DPOP(L)-A-1